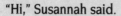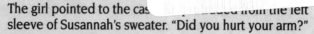
"Hi," Susannah said.

The girl pointed to the cas̶t̶ ̶t̶h̶a̶t̶ ̶p̶r̶o̶t̶r̶u̶d̶e̶d̶ from the left sleeve of Susannah's sweater. "Did you hurt your arm?"

"I broke my wrist."

"Does it hurt?" the child asked.

"Not so much now, but it did in the beginning. The doctor put this on to make it better." The girl kept staring at it, seemingly fascinated. "Would you like to see?"

She nodded, and Susannah pushed up her sweater. The cast covered her hand, except for her fingers and thumb, and went up to just below her elbow.

"How come you don't got any of your friends' names on it?"

"Well, that's a very good question. Do you think you could do it for me?"

Her eyes lit up. "Uh-huh. I even got a marker." Hastily she took off her backpack and rummaged around until she came up with two. She slowly and carefully wrote the name Nia in black. Instead of dotting the *i* she drew a red heart.

"How beautiful," Sussannah said. "Thank you."

Nia looked quickly over her shoulder, as if realizing she'd strayed too far from the person who'd brought her. "I got to go."

"Are you here with your mother?"

"My daddy. My mama's dead."

Dear Reader,

I wish you and your family a wonderful holiday. I'm so
pleased this month to bring you my first Christmas book.
I had great fun researching, particularly the customs and
history of the Cherokee in western North Carolina. The
mountains are spectacular, the people warm and generous.

My story is about Ryan Whitepath, a Cherokee and
talented artist…and Susannah Pelton, a woman who has
lost everyone she loves. I hope you'll enjoy the Cherokee
legends in this book, the language and the love story. I
think Ryan's "Nana" will tickle you, and his little daughter,
Nia, will steal your heart.

Happy reading—and Merry Christmas!

Fay Robinson

P.S. Write me at fayrobinson@mindspring.com. To learn
more about the research behind this book, please visit my
Web site at www.fayrobinson.com. Or come chat with me at
www.eHarlequin.com.

Books by Fay Robinson

HARLEQUIN SUPERROMANCE

911—A MAN LIKE MAC
961—COMING HOME TO YOU
1012—MR. AND MRS. WRONG
1068—THE NOTORIOUS MRS. WRIGHT

Christmas on Snowbird Mountain

Fay Robinson

HARLEQUIN®

TORONTO • NEW YORK • LONDON
AMSTERDAM • PARIS • SYDNEY • HAMBURG
STOCKHOLM • ATHENS • TOKYO • MILAN • MADRID
PRAGUE • WARSAW • BUDAPEST • AUCKLAND

ISBN 0-373-71094-1

CHRISTMAS ON SNOWBIRD MOUNTAIN

Visit us at www.eHarlequin.com

Printed in U.S.A.

For my mother…who was fearless.

And for Sherry, Brenda, Jackie and all the other
good sons and daughters taking care of elderly parents.

ACKNOWLEDGMENTS

I'd like to send my appreciation to the people of Graham County, North Carolina, the city of Robbinsville and the community of Snowbird for their hospitality and willingness to answer my questions. I also found the following works valuable in my research: *Snowbird Cherokees: People of Persistence* by Sharlotte Neely, The University of Georgia Press; *Meditations with the Cherokee: Prayers, Songs, and Stories of Healing and Harmony* by J. T. Garrett of the Eastern Band of the Cherokee, Bear and Company; *Medicine of the Cherokee: The Way of Right Relationship* by J. T. Garrett and Michael Tlanusta Garrett of the Eastern Band of the Cherokee, Bear and Company; *Another Country: Journeying Toward the Cherokee Mountains* by Christopher Camuto, The University of Georgia Press; *Aunt Mary Told Me a Story: A Collection of Cherokee Legends and Tales* as told by Mary Ulmer Chiltoskey, edited and compiled by Mary Regina Ulmer Galloway, North Carolina Publications; *Cherokee Plants: Their Uses—A 400 Year History* by Paul B. Hamel and Mary U. Chiltoskey, Cherokee Publications; *Cherokee Cooklore* by Mary and Goingback Chiltoskey, Cherokee Publications; *Walk in My Soul* by Lucia St. Clair Robson, Ballantine Books; *Beginning Cherokee* by Ruth Bradley Holmes and Betty Sharp Smith, University of Oklahoma Press; *Celebrate the Solstice: Honoring the Earth's Seasonal Rhythms Through Festival and Ceremony* by Richard Heinberg, Quest Books; *The Winter Solstice: The Sacred Traditions of Christmas* by John Matthews, Quest Books; *The Encyclopedia of Mosaic Techniques* by Emma Biggs, Running Press; *Mosaics* by Kaffe Fassett and Candace Bahouth, The Taunton Press; *Working with Tile* by Jim Barrett, Creative Homeowner; *Decorating with Tile* by Margaret Sabo Wills, Creative Homeowner and *Setting Tile* by Michael Byrne, The Taunton Press.

CHAPTER ONE

Fayetteville, West Virginia
Late October

SUSANNAH LOOKED DOWN into New River Gorge at the rapids nearly nine hundred feet below. Understanding why Native Americans had once called this the River of Death was easy. Even if you miraculously survived a fall here, you'd die on the boulders that dotted the banks, or face the possibility of being swept away in the cold, rushing water.

In the past twenty-three years, two men had drowned after jumps from the steel-spanned bridge where Susannah stood waiting to leap. A third had died when his pilot chute failed to open properly.

"Are you scared?" the older woman in front of her asked. Kay was her name. They'd met at last night's party and agreed to give each other moral support. Like Susannah, Kay was a first-timer.

"I'm a little uneasy," Susannah admitted, "but excited, too."

As far as jumps went, this wasn't one of the

worst. Another plus was that it was legal—at least for the next six hours during the annual Bridge Day event. Many other BASE jumps from natural and man-made structures had been outlawed in the U.S. The acronym stood for Building, Antenna, Span and Earth. Bridges and cliffs were two of the most popular places for take-offs.

But Susannah accepted the fact that, sanctioned by the National Park Service or not, flinging her body off a fixed object and plummeting toward the earth at more than forty miles an hour was dangerous, much more so than skydiving, another sport she'd taken up in the past year. The low altitude left little room for the deployment of a reserve chute if her main one failed. Her canopy or lines could also become tangled in the structure.

Even now rescue workers, or "trolls" as they'd been nicknamed, were below on the bridge supports, dangling like spiders from rappelling ropes.

Susannah wasn't worried so much about hitting a beam as she was overcoming the hazards of the landing. The designated area on the right shore was only a few meters wide, wooded and strewn with rocks.

She'd trained to land safely in wet places and water, her maneuvering skills were good and boats were positioned below to help if needed, but she remained a weak swimmer despite classes. A boat wasn't much help if you couldn't keep your head above water long enough for it to get to you.

The river was freezing and swollen from a week of hard rains, and setting down in it today was Susannah's option of last resort.

But she had to go through with this regardless of the danger, or rather *because* of the danger. During the nine years she'd taken care of her sick mother, she'd forgotten what it meant to feel carefree or excited. She certainly hadn't done anything adventurous.

"A good daughter." That was what the nurses had called her. Reliable. Sensible. Responsible. She was all those things and proud of it.

Alzheimer's, though, destroyed not only the patients but the people who loved them. That was what it had done to Susannah, devastated her emotionally. And now that her mother was gone, she felt a longing to be less reliable, less sensible and responsible. To be less *everything,* or at least different from the dull, unimaginative person she'd grown into.

She had the opportunity to live a different life and take chances—like with this jump—and she intended to do it.

If she chickened out, she might as well go back to the bleak existence she'd had until eighteen months ago, when her mother had died.

The new-and-improved Susannah wouldn't lose

her nerve. This person took risks. This person no longer had to worry about being suffocated by responsibility. Her new approach to life was simple: see everything, experience everything and never forget that each day might be her last.

She'd sold the house and quit her job as an office manager for a law firm in Waycross, Georgia. Anything that wouldn't fit under the camper shell of her new pickup truck she'd given away or taken to the Salvation Army.

In no particular order, she'd committed her desires to paper. Her *Life List,* as she called it, was a blueprint for happiness and fulfillment.

While the items changed and the list continued to grow, so far she'd gone for a dip with dolphins, run a marathon, raised money to protect the endangered black rhino, belly danced, helped Habitat For Humanity build a house for a low-income family and visited the capitals of thirteen states. Thirty-seven more to go.

She'd confronted her fear of heights by taking skydiving lessons, and said goodbye to a lifetime of claustrophobia by going on a three-day caving trip with a group of experienced spelunkers.

Growing her short auburn hair to her waist would take more time; so far, it had only reached her chin. And some of the things she dreamed of accomplishing—like performing in a ballet and being the star of a movie—were perhaps a bit too ambitious, but she wasn't discounting any possibility.

If she didn't at least try, she'd certainly never eat real French onion soup in Paris or dance the tango in Brazil. She'd never have wild, uninhibited sex with a handsome stranger.

The line moved forward more quickly than Susannah expected, bringing her focus back to *this* item on her list. She was among three hundred people awarded slots to jump today. The weather was fair and no one had experienced any problems yet. Soon it would be Susannah's turn.

Kay mumbled over her shoulder, "I don't think I can do this."

"If you don't, you'll lose your entry fee and the couple hundred more you spent on the adaptive rigging."

"Money I can replace," Kay told her. "My life I can't."

"Very true, and I don't want to push you into doing this if you're afraid, but you told me last night that you've been planning this for months and asked me to give you a nudge if you backed out. Didn't you say you begged your family to let you come?"

"Yes."

"If you don't follow through, how would you face them?"

"I'd face them just fine. My husband would be

relieved. He said I was crazy when I took up sky-diving last year, but when I told him I wanted to try this—'' she snorted ''—he said I'd gone completely nuts. I'm beginning to believe he's right.'' Nervousness had her chewing her fingernails. ''What insanity made you sign up?''

''I watched a TV program one night where BASE jumping was featured. The idea of it terrified me, so I knew I had to do it—you know, to prove I could.''

''You *are* insane.''

''Probably so, since I'm afraid of heights and I can't swim.''

''But you skydive. How can you do that if you're afraid of heights?''

''I don't know. I just force myself. I figure going ahead while being scared is better than hiding from the fear.''

Kay looked over the side and grimaced. ''*Hiding* is starting to sound pretty good to me right now. This seems a whole lot scarier than skydiving.''

''But that's the whole point, to do something a little off-the-wall, even if it's scary. If you weren't here, what else would you be doing?''

''I'd probably be raking leaves or cleaning house.''

''I bet this'll be more fun.''

''Yeah, you're right.'' Kay nodded, seemingly reassured, but when it came time for her to jump, she balked. "I can't," she said, scrambling down off the exit platform.

Some of the hundred thousand spectators around them began to boo.

"Come on," Susannah urged. "You said you wanted to add adventure to your dull life. Here's your chance."

"I know, but I was wrong. The truth is, I love my life. I have a great husband and two kids who need me and think I'm perfect. So what if I'm nearly forty, overweight and the most exciting thing I do all week is laundry? I can live with that." She squeezed Susannah's arm. "I'm sorry."

"It's okay. I understand." And she truly did. Kay had her family to think about. Susannah no longer had family, or anyone who mattered. She especially didn't have anyone who thought her perfect.

She'd been the only child of elderly parents, now both dead along with both sets of her grandparents. Her friends had all drifted away when her mother's Alzheimer's worsened and her behavior had become more bizarre.

Even Andrew, the man she'd planned to spend the rest of her life with, had abandoned her when she needed him most. He'd been unable to cope with having his needs placed behind those of a sick person.

At twenty-eight, Susannah was alone in the world.

If she died today, not a soul would care except this woman from Arkansas whose last name she didn't even know.

The crowd started to chant, urging Susannah into action. "Jump…jump…jump."

The official controlling the line gave her a hard look. "Are you going or not?"

"Yes, I'm going."

She climbed the platform straddling the bridge rails and visualized what she had to do once she took off. By arching her body and pointing her hips at the horizon, she could stay upright until the wind turned her naturally into a face-to-earth position. Two seconds into the freefall, she'd reach to the small of her back and grab her pilot chute, tossing it toward the sky.

If everything went right, the chute would unfurl and she'd feel the reassuring tug upward, when the canopy fills. And if it didn't, she'd be seven seconds away from death.

"Hey," she called out to Kay. "What's your last name?"

"Murphy. Yours?"

"Pelton."

"I enjoyed meeting you, Kay Murphy."

"Same here, Susannah Pelton. Have a great life."

"I plan to."

Susannah took a deep breath to shore up her resolve, and with three running steps, launched herself into the air.

Sitting Dog, North Carolina
One week later

THE ONLY SOUNDS in the forest were the faint chattering of the birds as they foraged for seeds and the crunch of Ryan Whitepath's boots in the snow.

He could have driven the four miles to the school bus stop to get Nia, but he preferred the half-mile shortcut down the mountain, where he could free his mind from the projects he had to finish this week.

Work was going well. Professionally and financially he was successful. He had more commissions than he could handle and three upcoming gallery shows featuring his handcrafted tiles and display mosaics. But the obligations of his career were keeping him inside too much lately, and his personal life had gone to hell.

Disconnected was a good description of how he felt. His once-strong connection with the earth, which had always brought him peace and was the very foundation of his art, had experienced a short circuit over the past year. He needed to restore it before his creativity suffered.

He missed the feel of the wind on his face and the way it carried the faint smell of wood smoke on a brisk day. He missed witnessing the change of seasons up close, the brilliance of fall fading to the gray of winter, then the revival of color in the spring and summer.

All this land, as far as he could see across the Snowbird and Unicoi ranges, had once been the home of the *Ani Yunwiya,* the Principal People, but the nine hundred acres his family owned now had come to them only fifty years ago.

His father had taught him about the mountains as a boy, the places where the deer wallow and the wild boar root, where caves exist that can hide a man forever and wild berries grow in such abundance that you never have to worry about hunger.

Such secrets, gifts from parent to child for count-less generations, were bonds to Elohi, Mother Earth, the Center. Ryan had neglected his obligation to pass along what he had learned to his daughter. Per-haps she felt disconnected, as well, and that was part of her problem.

She wouldn't like that he hadn't brought the truck, but maybe on the walk home they'd see wild turkeys or the pair of comical mink that had taken up residence near the stream, and it would make her smile. So little did these days.

The death of her mother from pancreatic cancer last March had been hard on the six-year-old, even though Nia had never lived with Carla nor visited her in London more than a handful of times.

Nia was experiencing what the therapist called Separation Anxiety Disorder. She'd lost one parent. Now she was afraid of losing the other.

Ryan had tried explaining about the eternity of the soul, that it's alive before it goes into the body and remains alive after it leaves, but she was too young to fully understand. So he'd sent her to psychologists to help her deal with the grief. After three months of meetings with one and then four months with a second, he couldn't see much progress. Nia remained confused and unhappy.

His vibrant, outgoing daughter was gone. In her place was a quiet child who cried for no reason and didn't want to be alone, sleep or even go to school.

The doctor had suggested trying drug therapy after Christmas to control the anxiety attacks that had begun in the last month, but the thought frightened him. Nia was only a baby. Medications carried risks, especially in someone so young.

He didn't know what to do. His grandmother counseled patience. She believed something besides Carla's death was bothering Nia.

Nana Sipsey had taken of the sacred tobacco one night and had a vision: a redbird with a broken wing would heal his child's heart and, in so doing, heal itself.

Ryan hadn't voiced his skepticism, but it existed. His grandmother came from a long line of healers of the *Ani Wodi,* the Red Paint Clan. He trusted her knowledge of medicines for simple cures of headaches, colds and such.

Accepting prophecy was difficult for him, though, especially when something as important as the emotional stability of his daughter was at stake.

Ahead, John Taylor's Trading Post came into view. The school bus pulled up outside just as Ryan left the woods.

This short stretch of road was the heart of Sitting Dog. A gas station-grocery store, an activities center and a volunteer fire station were the only buildings, but the eighty-four residents could find just about anything they needed, from tools to eggs, without driving the twenty miles to Robbinsville.

Their small community didn't have a McDonald's or a Blockbuster, but the store had videos for rent and its lunch counter served food that appealed to both Indians and whites.

A bank would be nice, but people who worked over on the reservation, Qualla Boundary, fifty miles to the northeast, took care of check cashing and deposits before driving home.

"Sa Sa," he called out, and Nia turned. She'd gotten off the bus with two friends who lived nearby, Iva Williams and Mary Throwing Stick.

"Hi, girls," he said as he walked up. "How was school?"

Mary answered for them. "Buddy Henderson brought his tonsils in a jar and made Iva sick. It was so gross."

"I didn't puke, though," Iva said proudly.

Ryan tried not to laugh, but it was impossible. "I'm glad to hear it." He pulled Mary's braid. "You didn't puke on anybody, did you, Pretty Miss Mary?"

She giggled and wrinkled her nose. "Uh-uh."

"Nia, how was your day?"

Nia shrugged and didn't say anything. Ryan didn't press. Simply getting her to *go* to school this morning had been a triumph. He was thankful she'd made it through the day without coming down with one of her stomachaches or headaches.

"How's your dog?" Ryan asked Mary. "Did she have her puppies yet?"

"Six of them. All black. Can Nia come by for a minute and see them?"

"Maybe another day." Darkness would fall soon and he still needed to recheck a couple of measurements at the activities center before the trek home. Workers were building an addition to use as a child care center and small library. Ryan had promised to complete a wall mosaic in time for the reopening, during the Christian holiday next month, and he was sorely behind. "I'll bring Nia to visit this weekend, Mary. We have chores to do right now."

"Can she come to my slumber party on Saturday? Iva's coming. And Tracie. And Kimberly. And..." She rattled off the names of ten or more little girls in their class. They were going to make banana splits and play games, she added with excitement.

Nia didn't jump in and beg to go, so Ryan hedged. "We'll see. Her grandmother might have other plans for her. She can let you know tomorrow."

The girls' mothers arrived to drive them home, and Nia finally spoke, telling her friends goodbye.

Once they were alone, Ryan tried to talk to her about her reluctance to attend the sleep-over party. "Sounds like a lot of fun, doesn't it?"

"I guess so."

"You like Mary. And all your friends will be there. Don't you want to go?"

"I want to stay home with you."

Ryan didn't push it. When she didn't want to do something, no amount of cajoling would work. She was like her mother in that respect. In the few months he'd dated Carla, he'd learned two things: to let her have her way and to leave her alone when she curled up inside herself.

"I need to go into the center for a few minutes," he told Nia. "Do you want to come with me or wait in John Taylor's where it's warmer? You can buy some paper to practice your writing.''

The buildings were adjacent. She'd be safe in the trading post among his neighbors. And it would be good for her to go in by herself.

"Can I go with you?" she asked.

"The heat's turned down, since there aren't any activities today. You'd be cold."

She looked around. "Can't I stay in the truck?"

"I came down the trail today."

"We got to walk in the snow?"

"Walking is good for you, and the snow's not deep. Besides, I told your grandmother and Nana Sipsey I'd see if I could find some possum wood grapes for a pie. You can help me pick them."

"But...the dark might get us. Or we could get lost."

"We'll be home by nightfall." His answer didn't seem to reassure her. He knelt down. "Hey, I'd never let anything hurt you. I know every inch of these woods."

"What if we meet a bear?"

"Mr. Bear is probably sleeping right now. He's snoring in his cave."

"But he could hear us and wake up."

"I'll wrestle him if he does."

"He might bite you."

"I'll bite him back."

She smiled a tiny bit. "Oh, Daddy."

"Will you go into the store? Show Daddy what a big girl you are and buy the paper yourself."

"I'm scared to."

"Remember what Dr. Thompson said. When something scares you, ask yourself why. What do you think's in there that can hurt you?"

"I don't know," she said with a shrug.

"You've known John Taylor and his wife since you were a little baby, and you've been in the store hundreds of times. Nothing in there will hurt you."

"You come, too."

"You can do it by yourself."

Her frightened little face almost made him cave in.

"Will you try, sweetheart?"

She nodded.

He walked her to the front door and gave her money, enough to buy some gum and a pad of paper.

"Stay inside. Don't leave the building for any reason. I'll come for you in a few minutes. I promise everything will be okay."

He said a silent prayer as she let go of his hand and went into the store alone.

CHAPTER TWO

SUSANNAH PARKED the truck at the pumps, filled the tank and checked the tires. This area here was beautiful, like a Christmas card scene. Snow frosted the branches of the trees and a blue mist veiled the mountains in the distance, making them seem painted.

Despite the beauty, driving the winding roads in icy conditions had made her tense. She was tired and hungry and her thermos was empty. A cup of hot coffee and a sandwich would be heaven. She also needed to get directions to see how far she was from Sitting Dog and the studio of the artist she wanted to talk to. She hoped he gave lessons. If he'd work with her, she might be able to mark another item off her list.

First, though, she had to find a place to stay for the night. When possible, and to save money, she stopped at RV parks and slept on the truck seat or used her sleeping bag in the back, under the camper. Tonight would be too cold for that. She'd have to squeeze money out of her tight budget for a motel room.

Well, at least she'd be able to take a hot shower. That alone was worth the extra expense.

Sleeping in a real bed and being able to go online to update her Web site were other pluses of a night indoors. Her travel diary, or ''Web log'' as the people on the Internet preferred to call it, was getting more than a hundred thousand hits a month from visitors signing on to read about her adventures.

Cranking the truck, she pulled away from the pumps so others could use them. She found a parking space in front of the store.

The warmth of the store was welcome. The building, much larger than it looked from outside, had three parts. The entry room held groceries, clothing and household items. At the back were two doorways. Through one was a self-service laundry. The other appeared to be a small restaurant.

Four old men sat near a gas heater playing a game with rectangular blocks. Cherokee, she guessed they were. Full-blooded or close to it.

She'd seen photographs of Native Americans, but had met very few in person. She hadn't imagined them to be so beautiful or their faces to hold so much expression.

Her fingers itched to get her art pad out of the truck and sketch them, but as a stranger in this isolated place she was already the center of attention. Everyone had turned to look at her as she walked in. They continued to stare as she picked up toothpaste and deodorant and walked to the cash register.

"Hello," she said brightly to the men. She gave them her warmest smile.

A man in a brown shirt threw up his hand in response and smiled back. "Welcome."

"Thank you." After paying for the gas and toiletries, she went to the rest room to freshen up and wandered over to the restaurant to have a look at what they offered. She took a seat at the counter, where one large woman seemed to be both taking orders and fixing meals. Bitsy, as one of the other patrons called her, had to weigh three hundred pounds.

"What would you like?" she asked.

"I'd love a cup of coffee. And do you have soup or sandwiches?"

"Both. I have ham, turkey, barbecued pork or venison sandwiches. Pumpkin soup, walnut, tomato or chicken noodle, all homemade. If you want a hot dinner, your choices are vegetables, hamburger steak or chicken gizzards." She handed her a small chalkboard that listed the vegetables; many were traditional and some—like ramps—Susannah had never heard of.

She wavered between being adventurous and satisfying her hunger.

"I'd like to try something exotic, but I'm also starving and don't want to order and then not like what you bring. Any suggestions for something unique, but that I'll probably enjoy?"

"What are you leaning toward?"

"Well, definitely not the gizzards, but the venison sounds intriguing. And the pumpkin soup. And the walnut soup. But, then again, ham I know I like. Maybe I should play it safe."

"I can make you a half ham, half deer meat sandwich and put the two kinds of soup in small cups instead of bowls so you can have a taste of both for the same price. And I make a nice bean bread that goes well with soup."

"Oh, sounds perfect."

"It'll be right up."

"Can you also tell me how far it is to Sitting Dog?"

"You're here."

"But where's the *town?*"

"You're smack-dab in the middle of it. If you want a town, then Robbinsville, fifteen or twenty miles to the northeast, is the place to head. They've got, oh, maybe seven hundred folks."

"That doesn't sound like much of a town."

"Sugar, you're in Graham County. We've got

plenty of mountains, creeks and trees, but we're way short on people. Only about eight thousand of us are crazy enough to live here.''

''In the whole county?''

''Yep. The land's mostly government-owned national forest. We're the only county in North Carolina that doesn't even have a four-lane road.''

''I passed through some of the forest land. I went nearly fifty miles without seeing another car.''

''Which way did you come in?''

''From Tellico Plains, Tennessee, over the Cherohala Skyway.''

''Lord, girl! You took a chance in this weather. That's a desolate trip this time of the year, and this early snow must've made the going even tougher. Some of those curves never get enough sun to melt the ice.''

''The scenery was worth it. I've never seen anything more beautiful in my life.''

''It *is* pretty.''

''Is there a motel close by?''

''No, sorry. We don't get many tourists this late in the year. In warm weather we attract nature lovers who hike the back country, but they mostly camp out.''

''I imagine with this fresh snowfall everyone's farther upstate at the ski resorts.''

''Probably. We don't normally get our first snowfall for a couple more weeks, so I'm sure the skiers have headed up to Maggie Valley. But they're missing a treat. These mountains are the place to be in winter, especially during the holidays.'' She refilled the coffee of a man two seats down. ''You only passing through?'' she asked Susannah.

''I'm not sure yet. Do you have a bed-and-breakfast? Even a boardinghouse would do.''

''A couple B-and-Bs. And there's a lodge, but they're probably closed for the season and won't open up again until late March or mid-April. When you've finished eating, you can borrow my phone book and call around. Maybe someone around here is open.''

''Thanks. I appreciate that.''

Several people sat down to order and the woman got busy filling orders. The venison she brought Susannah a few minutes later was delicious, the pumpkin and walnut soups interesting. The best part was the bread—simply out of this world. Susannah was glad she'd taken a chance on something different.

She was finishing her coffee when she felt a presence. She glanced to her side and found a young girl with huge brown eyes staring up at her.

''Hi,'' Susannah said.

''*Si yo*,'' the girl answered. Her front teeth on the top and bottom were missing, making her whistle slightly when she talked.

"I'm sorry. I don't speak your language."

"I said hello."

"Oh, well, then *si yo* to you, too."

The girl pointed to the cast that protruded from the left sleeve of Susannah's sweater. "Did you hurt your arm?"

"I broke my wrist."

"How?"

"Mm, I guess you could say I tried to fly and found out I wasn't any good at it."

Actually, the flying part had gone well. She'd jumped from the bridge, her chute had opened perfectly and she'd drifted down toward the landing area without problems. At the last second the wind had shifted. In an attempt to stay out of the water, Susannah had overcompensated and hit the rocks.

"Does it hurt?" the child asked.

"Not so much now, but it did in the beginning. The doctor put this on to make it better." The girl kept staring at it, seemingly fascinated. "Would you like to see?"

She nodded.

Susannah turned on the stool and pushed up her sweater. The cast covered her hand, except for her fingers and thumb, and went up to below her elbow.

"It's white. My friend Iva broke her arm last year and her thing was purple."

"That's because this one's made out of plaster.

Your friend Iva's was probably made out of fiberglass and those come in purple and other colors.''

"How come you didn't get a pretty one?" She reached out and lightly rubbed her fingers over it.

"Because the pretty ones cost a lot more money and I was being frugal."

"Fruit girl?"

"Frugal," Susannah repeated with a smile. "That means I was trying not to spend too much money."

"How come you don't got any of your friends' names on it?"

"Well, that's a very good question." And one Susannah didn't know how to answer for a child. How did you explain to someone her age that you didn't have any friends? Fortunately she didn't have to.

"We printed our names on Iva's," the girl said, forging ahead. "I put mine right there." She placed her index finger in the middle of Susannah's forearm.

"That sounds pretty."

"I could only print then, but I can write my name in cursive now." She looked up with expectation, her sweet face showing exactly what she longed to do. "I can write it real good."

"You can already write in cursive? Goodness. How old are you?"

"*Sudali.*" She held up six fingers.

"Well, this must be my lucky day because I've been looking all over for a six-year-old to write her name on my cast and couldn't find one. Do you think you could do it for me?"

Her eyes lit up. "Uh-huh. I even got a marker." Hastily she took off her school backpack and rummaged around until she came out with two. Susannah held her arm steady in her lap while the girl slowly and carefully wrote the name *Nia* in black. Instead of dotting the *I* she drew a red heart.

"How beautiful. Thank you."

"You won't wash it off?"

"No."

"Promise?"

"I promise." The cast would be removed and thrown away in four to six weeks, but the child probably hadn't thought about that.

Nia looked quickly over her shoulder, as if realizing she'd strayed too far from the person who'd brought her. "I got to go." She returned her things to her pack.

"Are you here with your mother?"

"My daddy. My mama's dead. She got the cancer in her stomach."

"I'm sorry."

"You got a mama?"

"No, not anymore."

"Did she get the cancer?"

"Something like that."

"Do you miss her?"

"Very much."

"You got a daddy?"

"No, I'm afraid not."

"Who tucks you in at night?"

"I…" The question sent a sharp pain through Susannah's heart. "I tuck myself in."

"My daddy tucks me in. I got a Gran and a Nana Sipsey to help."

"Then I'd say you're a very lucky little girl to have so many people who love you."

The child said goodbye and left. Susannah ordered another cup of coffee. "Anything else?" the waitress asked when she'd finished.

"No, thanks. Everything was delicious."

"Glad you enjoyed it. Want that phone book now?"

"Yes, please." Susannah paid for her meal, then Bitsy helped her look up numbers for places where she might stay the night. She wrote them down.

While she had the book, she flipped over to the *W* section and skimmed the listings.

"Do you know Ryan Whitepath, the artist? This lists only a post office address and I'd like to drop by and speak to him."

"Sure. Everybody knows the Whitepaths.

They've lived here all their lives. That was Ryan's little girl you were talking to."

"You're kidding!"

"He usually picks her up out front when she gets off the school bus. Hurry and you might catch him."

Susannah raced through the store and outside. She scanned the parking lot for Nia, but didn't see her anywhere. Damn! So close to Whitepath and she'd missed him.

The one item on her Life List that had caused her the most concern was "Create something beautiful and lasting." For months she'd pondered what that should be and the training she needed to accomplish it. A painting maybe? An exquisite photograph? A sculpture? None of those things seemed exactly right, but she couldn't explain why. She wanted the whatever she made to be admired long after she died, but it also had to "speak" to her heart, to be part of her somehow.

While waiting in the emergency room in Fayetteville to have her wrist set, she'd wandered off in search of a rest room and wound up in the lobby for the recently completed heart center. The floor had been the most stunning mosaic she'd ever seen, hundreds of thousands of tiny pieces of tile expertly placed so that they gave the illusion of walking on a leafy forest floor in autumn. Looking at it had literally taken her breath away.

A pamphlet about the heart center credited the work to Cherokee artist Ryan Whitepath of Sitting Dog, North Carolina.

A mosaic. Perfect! They were beautiful and durable. She'd found out on the Internet that one dating back thirty-five hundred years had recently been uncovered by archaeologists and was still intact.

She believed she had the talent to learn the craft. She'd started college as an art major, planning to be a portrait painter. Her mother's illness had killed that dream the following year, but in the last few months she'd taken up drawing again.

She possessed a sense of color and understood perspective. And it wasn't as if she wanted to be an expert, only make a little piece of something Ryan Whitepath could insert in a larger work. *If* she could talk him into giving her lessons and letting her help in his studio.

That request, she felt, was best made in person rather than by telephone. So she'd rearranged her schedule and backtracked into North Carolina.

The timing was perfect. She planned to be in New York City to watch the ball drop in Times Square on New Year's Eve. That gave her eight weeks before she had to move on.

She reentered the store and went back to the lunch counter. "I wasn't quick enough. Can you tell me how to get to Mr. Whitepath's studio or home?"

"Be glad to." The waitress picked up a napkin and started drawing a map. "I hope you have four-wheel drive."

RYAN ENJOYED the walk back, but Nia struggled to keep up. He put her on his shoulders and carried her.

"Am I heavy, Daddy?" she asked in *Tsalagi*.

"Yes, you're heavy. And you squirm like a trout. I can hardly hold on to you."

She wriggled her behind, teasing him. "There was a lady with pretty hair in the store. She tried to fly and fell down and hurt herself."

"She tried to fly in the store?"

"No, Daddy, not in the *store*." She giggled, a welcome sound.

"Was she an eagle?"

"Uh-uh."

"A big owl?"

"No."

"A moth?"

"No!"

"Maybe she was a goose like you, Sa Sa."

"No, silly. She was a *lady*."

They came to the possum wood trees, persimmons some people called them. He set Nia on the ground and took a sack from his jacket pocket to hold their bounty. Deer and raccoons considered the tart fruit a treat, and the many tracks in the snow told him the animals had already found the ripe ones that had fallen.

"Help me dig down and get some good ones for a pie. The cold will have turned them sweet."

They gathered enough for several pies, along with a few large pinecones Nia wanted to use for a Thanksgiving project at school. Few Indian families celebrated the holiday, but Nia, like all children in this area, went to the county school where such things were usual.

He and Nia thanked the earth for the possum wood berries and pinecones and then started back up the trail.

"We made it before the dark got us, Daddy," Nia said as the house came into view.

"And I didn't have to wrestle a single bear."

Ryan didn't stop at his place. A few years ago he'd converted the old equipment barn from his father's defunct furniture-making business into a modern workshop with two kilns in the back and living quarters in the loft for him and Nia, but Nia most often ate in the house and sometimes slept there. Ryan did, too, unless he worked late, which was happening more often than he liked.

A vehicle he didn't recognize was parked in the yard. "We have company."

"Is it Uncle Joe?"

"No, not unless he's bought a new truck." That wasn't likely. His youngest brother didn't have money for luxuries. Joseph was a carpenter and furniture maker and worked hard, but employment opportunities were limited in the sparsely populated county. Most of the land was virgin forest. Only six percent was appropriate for cultivation. Except for one factory, they had no industry.

Just inside the door, he helped Nia take off her boots and coat. He followed her through the house to the kitchen.

A pretty young woman with red hair sat at the table with his mother and grandmother drinking tea. "You're here!" Nia exclaimed. To his amazement, she rushed over and climbed into the stranger's lap.

"Hi, sweetheart." The woman playfully tugged on one of Nia's long braids.

"Look, Daddy! I wrote my name on her arm."

Nia badgered the woman into pushing up the sleeve of her sweater to reveal a cast with her signature.

Ryan couldn't have been more stunned. The fiery hair. The broken "wing."

His grandmother nodded to him with a satisfied smile. "Rejoice," she said in their native tongue. "The redbird has come."

CHAPTER THREE

RYAN WHITEPATH hadn't moved or said a word since he arrived. He stood in the doorway holding a sack and stared at Susannah as if she had a second head. She stared back. Not that it was a hardship. On the contrary, she was having a difficult time dragging her eyes away.

The man was extraordinary looking, with black hair falling in shiny soft waves past his shoulders, and rugged, almost harsh, features. If not for the flannel shirt and jeans, he could've stepped out of a nineteenth-century painting by Frederic Remington, or been the model for Maynard Dixon's warrior in *The Medicine Robe*.

"The woman wishes to speak to you about your art, Ryan," his mother said. Mrs. Whitepath had offered Susannah a sweet, herbal tea and kept her entertained while they waited for her son and granddaughter to come home.

The older woman—eighty, at least, and no bigger than a twig—was the other woman's widowed mother-in-law, Sipsey Whitepath, the "Nana Sipsey'' Nia had mentioned. She spoke Cherokee and broken English, which meant she was sometimes hard to understand. She also acted as if Susannah had been expected, and that made her a bit uncomfortable.

"Hi," Susannah said to the man. "I was at the store earlier and met Nia, but I didn't realize she was your daughter."

"Who did you say you are?"

"I'm sorry. I should've introduced myself. My name is Susannah Pelton."

He put his sack down on the table. Instead of sitting, he chose to lean with his back against the counter and his arms crossed over an impressive set of chest muscles.

"And you're from where?" he asked.

"Originally Waycross, Georgia, but the last year or so not from anywhere in particular. I've been traveling the country." She took the hospital pamphlet out of her purse and passed it to his mother who, in turn, handed it to him. "I saw the floor you did for the hospital in Fayetteville, West Virginia, and thought it was exquisite. I was wondering if you'd consider giving me lessons in designing and creating mosaics. I have a couple of months of free time and I'm eager to learn."

"You drove three-hundred miles to ask me that?"

"And to see more of your work, of course, if it wouldn't be an imposition."

"I'm sorry, Miss Pelton. If you'd called I could have saved you the trouble of a trip. I don't give lessons."

"Not ever?"

"Occasionally in the summer months I take on an intern from one of the universities, but right now I have too much to do and too little time to do it in. I can't possibly work with anyone who has no prior experience."

"I'll gladly pay you." She'd already calculated what she could afford, not much, but this was so important she was prepared to dip into her emergency fund.

"Money's not the issue," Whitepath said. "I can't give you lessons. I'm overwhelmed with contracts and it's going to take every free minute I have to fulfill them. In fact, I should be working right now."

"I see." Susannah's hope dimmed. "Won't you make an exception this one time? I've taken art classes and I have a sketchbook in my truck with examples of my work."

"I'm sorry. Like I said, I'm too busy to train anyone. It would only put me further behind."

"I believe I could be a help to you rather than a hindrance."

"With a broken arm?"

"The break isn't severe."

"How did you do it?"

Nia piped up, "She tried to fly, Daddy. I told you."

"*Did* you try to fly?" he asked.

"I jumped off a bridge using a parachute," Susannah explained. "It feels a bit like flying. My landing was off, though, and I hit some rocks."

He grunted and she could hear censure in it. He thought her a fool for doing something so ridiculous.

"I'm sorry you came this far for nothing, but I can't help you." He pushed away from the counter. Apparently he'd decided his discussion with Susannah was over. "Nia, do you have homework?"

"I got to read aloud. And I got to look up ten words in my dictionary."

"Let's do it before it's too late. Go wash your hands so you won't get the book dirty."

"Can I read to the pretty lady?" She cocked her head and exchanged smiles with Susannah. Again, Whitepath's gaze seemed puzzled, as if Susannah had said or done something peculiar.

"We'll see. Go wash your hands, goosey. Be a good girl. Find a book you'd like to try."

His expression softened when he spoke to his child, making him look different. Susannah wouldn't say *handsome* because it didn't fit. *Less severe* was more accurate.

Nia scooted off Susannah's lap. When she'd left the room, the older woman mumbled a few words in Cherokee. That prompted a quick response from Whitepath. Judging by his scowl, his grandmother had clearly said something he didn't want to hear.

"Ryan, don't be rude," his mother admonished. She turned to Susannah. "Forgive my son. He forgets not all people speak *Tsalagi*."

"Sorry, Miss Pelton. I didn't mean to exclude you."

"Call me Susannah, please."

"Susannah."

She'd never liked her name, but it sounded... appealing coming from his lips. Pleasurable, like the brush of silk against her skin.

"Don't apologize," she told him. "I love listening to your language being spoken. I wish I'd bought some books so I could learn a few basic phrases. *Tsalagi*." Susannah pronounced it slowly. "I assume that means Cherokee?"

"Yes, the word refers to our language and is one of only a few common to Cherokee here and out west."

"I don't understand. You speak a different language from other Cherokees?"

"A different *dialect*."

His mother jumped in and explained. "The Eastern Band is a separate entity from the Cherokee Nation in Oklahoma. Most Cherokee here in North Carolina and surrounding states speak *Atali* and those in Oklahoma *Kituhwa*. We in Sitting Dog, however, have a mixed dialect that's not really used on the nearby reservation. I'm afraid a book of phrases would do you little good. You must hear the language spoken, the subtleties of it, to truly understand the meaning of the words."

"Why is there a difference in dialects if the reservation is so close?"

"We've been isolated from each other until recent years because of the mountains. Traditions and lifestyles have evolved differently, as well. Like Qualla Boundary, we have a few mixed-race families because we've lived among our white neighbors for many years, but most of our residents are full-blooded. English is our *second* language rather than our first. We speak mostly *Kituhwa,* as our ancestors did centuries ago. The dialect is similar to that once spoken by the Cherokee who were relocated to Oklahoma, but with colloquial differences. We borrow from both the Eastern and Western dialects."

"Well, it's lovely. Very musical."

"Yes, a good description. That's why we so often express ourselves through song."

"Is Nia fluent in *Tsalagi* and English?"

"She speaks both and is learning to read and write both. She's been brought up to learn and respect the language and customs of both races. Her mother was white."

Susannah had thought so. The child's skin was light, not dark like her father's. Her hair was a warm brown rather than black. She could pass for white or Native American.

"Nia mentioned that her mother had passed away. I'm very sorry."

Whitepath made a strangled sound. He straightened, taking several steps toward her. "She told you that?"

"She said her mother died of cancer."

He and his mother stared at her strangely again. His grandmother only nodded, as if she wasn't surprised.

"I'm sorry," Susannah said. "Was talking to her about it a mistake? If I did something wrong, I apologize."

"No, no," Mrs. Whitepath said. "You did nothing wrong. We're only amazed that Nia confided in anyone. She's rarely so open with strangers, and she never speaks about her mother. She seems to have taken a great liking to you, though. That's what Ryan and his grandmother were discussing."

"I see," Susannah said, but she suspected there was more to it than that. There was some kind of conflict between the man and the old woman. Sipsey Whitepath seemed pleased, but Ryan looked downright unhappy.

AT HIS MOTHER'S insistence and to Susannah's delight, Ryan Whitepath agreed to take her on a quick tour of his studio.

"I'll help Nia with her words while you're gone," his mother told him, ushering them out the front door with their coats.

They stood on the steps to appreciate the beauty of the landscape. The old house and its outbuildings sat about halfway up a mountain in a small clearing bordered by hardwoods and evergreens. A panorama of hills and valleys stretched out before them. Dusk had arrived, turning the trees to dark figures and streaking the sky with multiple shades of orange and pink. The scene was breathtaking.

"My God," Susannah said with a long sigh. "Everything seems too beautiful to be real."

"The sunrises are just as spectacular. And when a storm rolls through…it's like nothing else you can imagine."

"Have you always lived here, Mr. Whitepath? In these mountains, I mean."

"Call me Ryan. And yes, I've lived in the mountains and, for the most part, in this house all my life, except for the years I was away at school. I was born in one of the back rooms. So were my father, uncle, two younger brothers and my sister. My grandmother delivered all of us.''

"Do your siblings live in Sitting Dog?"

"Joseph does. Charlie's in Winston-Salem and Anita's a sophomore at the University of North Carolina at Asheville.''

"Is that where you went to school, UNC?"

"I did my undergraduate studies there in painting, but I was lucky enough to get a couple of corporate grants that allowed me to do graduate work in Ravenna, Italy, at The School of Mosaic Restoration.''

"I'm impressed."

"For my family it was a very big deal, since I was the first Whitepath to ever go to college—actually, the first to even graduate from high school.''

"Really? But your mother seems so well educated.''

"Because she works hard to improve herself. She's become an expert on the history of our people. She's also one of the founders of a national project to make sure every child has the opportunity to learn his or her native language.''

"That's ambitious."

"But important. Fewer than 150 native languages in the U.S. have survived out of several thousand, and we've already lost a major dialect of Cherokee called *Elati.* She's determined not to let that happen again.''

"I admire her for preserving your heritage.''

"I do, too. Because of her, I know who my ancestors are. That's important to me, to my understanding of who I am.''

"What about your father? Is he Cherokee?''

"Yes. His great-great-great-grandparents hid out in these mountains and eluded the soldiers who came in 1838 to relocate them. Their son was born later that year. They named him *Numma hi tsune ga,* Whitepath, after a chief of the same name from North Georgia who was a half-blood brother to Sequoyah. Chief Whitepath tried to warn against the government's treachery. But he wasn't successful at rousing the tribal elders to take a stand and was among those rounded up and marched west. Old and sick, he was one of the four thousand who died.''

"The Trail of Tears. I remember reading about it in my American History classes.''

"My family carries Chief Whitepath's name in remembrance of what he tried to do. We adopted it around 1900 as a surname.''

"Does it mean anything?''

"To an Indian, everything has a meaning. The *white path* is the path of happiness in the Green Corn Dance ceremony our ancestors practiced. For a Cherokee of the old time to say he was *white* meant he was taking the path of happiness, of peace.''

"So where does *Ryan* come from? That's obviously not Cherokee.''

"Ryan MacDougal was a childhood friend of my mother's who died in a fall. She named me for him. These mountains are full of families with Scottish and Irish heritage. You'll notice the cross-influences in the languages. Our legends are similar, too. Ever heard of the Little People from Irish folktales?''

"Of course. They're leprechauns. When I was little, I believed they lived in our den.''

"The Cherokee also know of the Little People, the good and bad spirits who inhabit the forest. The Little People are said to take things or move them. Sometimes they'll leave you a gift, and you're expected to reciprocate. My father used to swear they were constantly moving his tools.''

"What does your father do?''

"He used to run a shop here on the property with my grandfather and uncle. They made furniture. For the past fifteen years, he's lived in a little town called Lineville and worked for a trucking company. He and my mother are divorced.''

"Sorry,'' she said with a grimace. "I assumed your dad was at work. Am I being too nosy? I find your family fascinating.''

"No, no problem. The breakup was economic

more than anything. The business wasn't profitable anymore, so after Granddaddy died, my dad wanted to move to the city. My mother didn't. At first he was pretty good about coming home on weekends and holidays, and they tried to keep the marriage going. But over time the visits got more infrequent and then stopped. I haven't seen him in three or four years.''

"That has to be tough.''

"Everyone took it hard when he moved out, especially my brother Joe who was only seven and particularly close to him.''

"How old were you?''

"Fifteen. I'm the oldest.''

"So that made you the man of the house?''

He shrugged as if it were no big deal, but Susannah didn't believe that. Fifteen—thrust into adulthood... The situation must've been difficult for him.

He walked down the steps and motioned for her to follow.

"Get your sketchbook and I'll look at it,'' he said, striding over to her truck.

"You mean you might reconsider teaching me?''

"No, but if you want my opinion on your work, I'll give it.''

WITH HER SKETCHBOOK under her arm, Susannah fell in next to him, trying to keep up with his long strides as they made their way down the driveway. She thought he'd head to a cabin on the right, but instead he turned left toward a long barn.

"My studio's over there," he said.

The air was crisp and smelled of sawdust, and in the fading light she could see piles of the stuff rotting behind the building. Snow had begun to fall again.

"This used to be my dad's workshop," Ryan explained. The long structure had double barn doors in the middle and a regular door to the left, with an opening below for a pet to go in and out. He opened the smaller door and they went inside. "I needed a large space nearby so I closed in the sides, added plumbing and a floor and made a workshop and apartment."

Susannah had expected something rustic and dark, considering the exterior, but when he flipped on the lights, she couldn't hold back her surprise. The interior was spacious and airy, as modern as any dwelling in a big city.

"Wow! This is wonderful."

"It works well for the business and for me personally. I'm close enough to take care of my mother and grandmother and for them to help me with Nia, but I have my own space and privacy. At least, I feel the illusion of privacy."

The main floor was his workshop. Long plywood

tables made an L along one side and across the back, holding projects in various states of completion. Sketches and vibrant paintings covered the walls. The stairs on the left led to a loft where he lived.

He showed her around the main floor. Shelves under the tables held glass jars filled with tiny tiles of every conceivable color and hue. Larger tiles were stacked in bins along the right wall.

"Do you use commercial tiles or make your own?" she asked, as they walked through the kiln room.

"Both. It depends on the project and what I'm trying to accomplish. If I can't get the color, texture or durability I'm looking for, I'll make my own. A good part of my business is restoration, which involves hand-making or painting tiles to match older or antique ones. I often have to experiment with pigments, glazes, bisques and firing techniques."

"You do all the work here?"

"Mostly. I create manageable sections of tile by attaching it to a special backing I designed myself. When the whole piece is done, I ship, reconstruct and install. I prefer to work from scratch on-site, but that's not practical because of the time and expense involved."

They came back to the main room and he showed her his office, in the corner area by the stairs. Papers were strewn haphazardly on his desk, as well as the light table. Everywhere, actually. The whole office needed a good tidying.

A white Persian cat lay stretched out on top of a tall bookcase, and it watched Susannah with eyes like gold jewels, expression haughty.

"Hello," Susannah called up. "What's your name?"

"That's Abigail," Ryan supplied. "I thought it would be good for Nia to learn responsibility for taking care of a living thing, but I have a suspicion Abigail owns us and we're *her* pets rather than the other way around."

"Cats can be a bit independent. She's so beautiful."

"She knows it, too."

He took Susannah's jacket and flung it over a chair, then shed his own. Grabbing a rubber band out of his desk drawer, he drew his dark hair off his face, into a ponytail.

"Do you wear your hair long because you're Native American?" Susannah asked.

"I prefer *Indian*."

"Sorry."

"That's okay. I'm not offended by *Native American*. The term is just a little too politically correct for me. Others like it, and that's fine. And to answer your question, no, I don't wear my hair long to appear more Indian. It's vanity. With short hair I look about twelve.''

She smiled at his honesty.

''I thought maybe you were trying to look authentic.''

''To do that, I'd have to cut it to stand up in a ridge along the back of my head down to my neck, and then shave the rest.''

She wrinkled her nose but didn't say anything.

''That was the style for Cherokee men before about 1800, except for the Long Hair or Twister Clan.''

''I don't think you'd look too good bald.''

''Neither do I.''

''I'm envious of how long and glossy your hair is. And the color's gorgeous.''

''I was just thinking the same thing about yours.''

He reached out and picked up a strand, gently rubbing it between his fingertips. She hardly breathed.

''To tsu hwa,'' he said softly.

''What?''

''Redbird.'' He must have realized he was still touching her, because he suddenly let the hair drop, thrusting both hands in the pockets of his jeans.

''Your grandmother called me that earlier.''

''Consider it an honor. The cardinal, or redbird, plays an important role in our legends.''

"How so?"

"It's revered by my people. There's a story behind how the bird got its color."

She waited, but he didn't go on. "Well, don't keep me in suspense."

"I can't tell the story like my grandmother can."

"Your grandmother's not here. Come on, don't leave me hanging."

Finally he acquiesced.

"Years ago the redbird wasn't red. He was plain and brown. One day, while gathering food for his family, he came upon a hurt wolf lying on a riverbank. The wolf had chased a raccoon up a tree and the raccoon had sneaked up on him while he was exhausted and plastered his eyes shut with mud. Thankful for the bird's compassion in helping him remove the mud, the wolf broke open a paint rock, a geode left from a volcanic eruption, and used it to give the bird a bright red coat. When the redbird flew home, his mate was so excited by his new color, she wanted some for herself. But she was afraid to leave their babies too long so she went and got only a little bit of the paint for herself. She was a good mother and hurried back to the nest. Today redbirds are symbols of beauty, kindness, compassion and dedication to family."

Susannah was thrilled to be compared to the little

bird. She'd always hated her hair color, but he'd made her see it in a whole new way.

"That was so lovely. How do you say 'redbird' again? *To-tso…*"

"*To tsu hwa.*"

"*To tsu hwa,*" she repeated several times until she'd memorized it. "Thank you for the story. I feel like…like I've been given a gift."

"You're welcome." He stared at her a moment longer than was healthy for her heart, then looked away. "I need to check my messages and return my calls. Do you mind?"

"No, go ahead. I'll wander about, if that's okay."

"Sure. On that table is a mosaic I'm repairing for a 1930s era pool, and over there's a ceiling I'm designing in conjunction with another company in California. The rest are…I don't know…different jobs and separate pieces for a museum show. Look all you want."

FIFTEEN MINUTES LATER, after reviewing his work and overhearing his telephone conversations, Susannah had decided that Ryan Whitepath was the most gifted person she'd ever met, but also the most disorganized.

She supposed his problem was a right brain, left brain thing, or that his overabundance of creativity had been offset by his lack of order.

His mosaics were brilliant, the colors earthy and the designs so stunning that Susannah felt spiritually changed just looking at them. But from a business standpoint, the man was hopeless.

He had no system for organizing his quotes and keeping up with correspondence, and apparently hadn't sent out invoices for work he'd completed weeks ago. The clutter on his desk made her cringe.

He tried to pull up a letter he'd typed on his computer to discuss with someone on the phone, but he couldn't find it. After several failed attempts, a lot of grumbling under his breath and the accidental deletion of a file, Susannah walked toward him.

"Here," she said, leaning over his shoulder. "Let me help before you do something you can't repair. What's the customer's name?"

"Health Systems of North Carolina." He spoke into the phone receiver. "Hold on a minute longer, Mr. Baker. We've almost got it."

She couldn't find a folder that resembled the name so she did a search and came up with one document called healthnc.doc.

"That's it," he said. He read off the figures to his customer and promised him an invoice within the week. When he'd ended the call, he asked Susannah how to print it, since he couldn't remember the procedure.

"You can go into your File menu and down to

Print, hit Control-P on your keyboard, or click on this icon on the toolbar. See how it looks like a little printer?''

He tried to print, but got an error message. "What the—? I did what you said."

She reached over and pushed a switch. "It helps if you turn on the printer."

"Oh, yeah. That makes sense."

She printed two copies. He seemed surprised when they actually came out into the tray. After, she used a utility program to retrieve the file he'd deleted and restore it to its original folder.

"Thanks for the help. I bought the computer expecting it to save me time. But I forget from one day to the next how to use it. Pretty stupid, huh?"

"Success takes practice."

"Nia's better at it than I am. It's downright embarrassing to have to ask a six-year-old for help when I do something wrong."

She cleared off a spot on the corner of his desk so she could sit.

"May I make a suggestion? You'd be able to find things more easily if you kept your quotes, correspondence and billing linked in this one program. It would also reduce your aggravation, especially at tax time."

"I don't know how to do all that. Typing a letter takes me two hours as it is, and then I can never find where I saved them—if I remember to save them."

"I could set up a billing system and teach you how to use it and your computer in exchange for a few mosaic lessons. Until I quit my job to travel, I ran an office for twenty-three attorneys. I'm proficient in all the software programs you have here, and I'm available for the next eight weeks. I could really have you rolling on this thing by Christmas. And I *know* that being more organized would save you a lot of time."

"Thanks for the offer, Susannah, but like I said earlier, I'm overwhelmed with contracts and I don't have time to train anyone. Or to learn anything new myself. On three separate occasions I've tried hiring office staff, but nobody worked out. Having someone nearby asking questions all the time proved to be too distracting. I couldn't concentrate."

Dispirited, she nonetheless couldn't blame him. "I understand."

"But let's take a look at your work. Maybe I can recommend someone else who can give you lessons."

He reached for the sketchbook she'd left propped against the chair holding her jacket, but she jumped up and grabbed it first. She clutched it to her chest. "I've changed my mind."

"Why?"

"Because I'm embarrassed. Your work is so incredible and mine, I realize now, is amateurish."

"With your enthusiasm, I doubt that. Where did you study?"

"I didn't, not really. I had a year of basic drawing classes at Auburn University and grand dreams of being a portrait artist, but then...well, something happened in my personal life that forced me to return home. I ended up getting a two-year business degree at a community college."

"How many years ago were those drawing classes?"

"Nine, unfortunately."

"That's a lot of time. Have you been drawing or painting since then?"

"Only sporadically. Recently I've started back in earnest, though."

"Let me see." He held out his hand. "I won't sugarcoat my opinion, but I'm rarely brutal."

With nervousness, Susannah gave up her art pad. He sat down in the office chair again while she reclaimed her former position on the edge of the desk.

He took his time examining each drawing, without making a comment about any of them. He'd flip a page, study for a minute or so, and then flip again.

Most of the drawings were of people she'd met in the past few months. Some were of her mother as she'd been before her illness, when she still remembered how to laugh and her eyes weren't clouded by confusion.

A piece of loose yellow paper fluttered from the pad to the floor when he turned a page, and Susannah realized with horror that it was her Life List.

Ryan picked it up, gave it a cursory look and stuck it in the back of the pad. He went on to the next drawing.

Thank you, God. She'd never intended anyone to ever see her desires so blatantly scribbled.

He closed the sketchbook and handed it to her. "Your drawings aren't bad. I wouldn't call them good, but considering that you haven't had a chance to develop your skills, you've done okay."

"So do I have any talent?"

"I see evidence of it. You probably won't ever be a professional artist, but with some practice you could develop into a gifted amateur."

"I'd be happy with that," she told him, pleased. "I'm really only drawing for myself. I don't expect to make a living at it."

"Then keep doing it. Draw what you like and do it often. You'll see a big improvement fairly soon."

"And what about mosaics and tile-making? Do you think I could learn the techniques?"

"I think so, although I warn you that crafting people in tile is extremely hard and that's the subject you seem to like drawing the most."

"Oh, I don't care what kind of design I do. A leaf or a cloud would satisfy me as long as whatever I make will be around for a long time."

He pulled out an address book, jotted down the names of teachers in the southeast and included phone numbers.

"Try some of these people." He passed her the list. "Tell them I recommended you."

"I will. Thanks for your help. And your honest opinion. It means a lot to me."

They put on their jackets. Outside, the temperature had dropped dramatically with the coming of the dark, but yard lights guided their way. The snow was now ice in the low spots of the gravel driveway. Walking was difficult; twice she slipped and nearly fell. Only Ryan's quick action saved her.

"You need real boots," he said, supporting her under her good arm. "Those designer things are worthless up here."

"I have sturdy boots in the truck, but I didn't expect to be hiking through a blizzard when I got dressed this morning."

"If you think this is a blizzard, you've never been in one."

When, for the third time, she nearly went down on her backside, Ryan cursed. He picked her up and kept walking as though she didn't weigh anything.

"What are you *doing?*"

"Keeping you from breaking another bone."

Susannah should have protested, but he was warm, his arms were strong and, oh boy, he smelled good. The scent was masculine, woodsy.

"Do you usually carry your guests?"

"Only the klutzy ones," he answered playfully. He smiled, and the transformation truly shocked her.

She'd been wrong before. The man was handsome as hell.

CHAPTER FOUR

"'…AND…mouse…and…' What's this word?" Nia asked.

"Cricket," the woman told her.

"'Cricket…carr-ie-d…'"

"Carried."

"'Carried…the pea…to…get…her. To-get… Together'!"

"Very good. You're an excellent reader."

Ryan watched the exchange from the other side of the kitchen table. After he and Susannah had returned to the house, he'd been put to work peeling potatoes for supper, penance ordered by his grandmother for sassing her earlier.

Nana Sipsey had threatened to take a hickory switch to his backside if he didn't watch his tongue. She'd do it, too, no matter that he was a grown man and outweighed her by seventy pounds.

He hadn't meant to be disrespectful, but he didn't share his grandmother's quick acceptance of this woman. *Susannah.* The name fit her. He'd never seen skin so creamy. Her eyes were as blue as a robin's egg.

She seemed nice, friendly. He'd enjoyed talking to her at his workshop. Still, she was a stranger, a drifter who had no more regard for her own safety than to throw herself off a bridge.

Going by the quick look he'd gotten at that list of hers, she had a skewed perspective on what was important in life, too. And Nia didn't need to get attached to someone who would inevitably leave.

Regardless of his grandmother's insistence that Susannah had been sent to heal his daughter, he was *not* allowing her to stay. She could be bad for Nia, and a distraction for him, as well.

They were alone in the kitchen except for Nia. His mother and grandmother had suspiciously disappeared to the second floor. Susannah looked up and her smile turned his insides liquid.

Pretty. Too pretty. He'd never get any work done if she was around.

"You've done a great job teaching Nia to read," she said. "You should be proud."

"The praise belongs to her. She learns quickly."

Nia touched Susannah's necklace. "Why is your ring here?"

"Because I outgrew it. My mother gave it to me when I was a little girl about your age. When it wouldn't fit anymore I put it on this chain so I could still wear it.''

"The blue rock is pretty.''

"That's a sapphire, my birthstone. I used to believe the ring was magic and would give me courage.''

Nia wanted to slip it on, but Ryan told her she couldn't. He was afraid she'd break the slender chain.

"Can we read another book?'' she asked Susannah.

"I'm sorry, sweetheart, but I need to be going. I enjoyed having you read this one to me, though. I don't think I've ever met a little girl who reads as well as you do.''

"When will you be back?''

"Well...'' She appealed to Ryan for help explaining.

"Susannah has to go home, Nia,'' he told his daughter. "She won't be back because she doesn't live around here.''

Nia wrinkled up her face, confused. "Where do you live?''

"I used to have a house in a state called Georgia, right below this one, but I don't anymore. I sold it because I wanted to sleep in different places, to travel and see new things.''

"Sleep here.''

"No, I can't do that."

"Daddy can tuck you in. You *said* you don't got nobody to tuck you in."

His gaze met Susannah's and her pale complexion flushed slightly.

"I can't stay, Nia."

"He gets the covers just right and everything. Please, please?"

"Nia," Ryan warned. "Don't pester Susannah. She's already told you she has to go."

"But I don't want her to." She slammed the book on the table, crossed her arms in defiance and stuck out her bottom lip. Her eyes narrowed.

"Nia," Ryan warned in a low voice.

Instead of apologizing, she knocked the book to the floor.

He ordered her to go to her room until she could behave better. She climbed off Susannah's lap and stomped down the hall in her socks, smacking her fist loudly against the wall because she couldn't make any noise with her feet. He made her come back and return the book to the table.

"Don't leave that room until I tell you to, young lady."

"You don't love me," she spat.

He knew she didn't believe it, but the words still broke his heart.

"I love you more than anything in this world, but

I don't like being around you when you act like this. Tell Susannah goodbye and that you're sorry for being so naughty.''

He wasn't sure she'd do it, but she finally whispered it through her tears. She ran off to her bedroom.

"Sorry about that," he said. "She's had a rough time lately. Normally she's a great kid."

"Did your wife die recently?"

"Carla wasn't my wife, only Nia's mother," he felt compelled to explain for some reason. "She died in March, not long after being diagnosed."

"Stomach cancer? I believe that's what Nia said."

"Actually it was her pancreas, but Nia calls it stomach. She's had trouble dealing with her mother's death, although Carla lived abroad and never had custody of her."

"I lost my mother last year, so I know some of what she's feeling. Healing takes time." Her expression turned sad. "I don't think it's possible for a child, regardless of age, to ever completely get over losing a parent."

"Was your mother's death from illness or accident?"

"Complications from Alzheimer's."

"I've heard that's really hard on a family. Emotionally. Financially. Physically."

"*Hard* doesn't even begin to describe it. Luckily my dad had done well in the plumbing business, and he and my mom invested wisely. Money wasn't a problem until the last couple of years of her life. The physical part, though, was very difficult."

"And the emotional part?"

"Devastating."

"How long was she ill?"

"Nine years."

"Damn! How did you deal with it?"

"Not easily, and probably not with much grace, but when you're in that kind of situation you do what you have to and hope it's enough. By the end of her life, my mother no longer knew who I was and had become abusive. That was really hard. She'd been a gentle, lovely person before, and the disease changed her."

"Is that the personal problem you mentioned, the one that caused you to leave school?"

"Yes. She needed me at home. I was all she had."

"Where was your dad?"

"Dad died of a heart attack when I was four. All I remember about him was that he had a loud laugh and kept butterscotch candies in his pockets for me. Growing up, it was just me and Mom."

"No brothers or sisters?"

She shook her head. "My parents didn't think

they could have children. They'd tried for nearly twenty years without success and were resigned to being childless, and then, surprise! When my mom was forty-two and my dad forty-eight, she suddenly found herself pregnant.''

"Were you and your mom close?''

"Very close.'' Her voice trembled. "She was my best friend. Watching her slowly die was the hardest thing I've ever had to do.''

He'd judged her too quickly. He'd assumed her to be flighty and irresponsible, but that didn't mesh with the portrait now forming—a daughter who had loved her mother and been willing to give up her dreams to take care of her.

She was on the verge of crying, and he felt guilty that his question had upset her. She recovered by glancing at her watch.

"Gosh, look at the time.'' She stood abruptly. "I need to go. I still have to find a place to stay.''

"You don't have one?''

"No, but the lady at the store gave me numbers for a couple of places. Do you mind if I use your phone to see if any of them has a room?''

"Go ahead.''

She discovered that all the guest houses in the area were closed for the season. Ryan told her the owners of one were good friends of his. He called and asked them to take in Susannah for tonight.

"You can follow me over," Ryan said. "Bascombe and Helen Miller's place is only a few minutes from here."

"I think I've already taken up enough of your time. I can find my way if you'll give me directions."

"I can't send you out in the dark alone. The roads are dangerous, particularly for someone who's unfamiliar with them and driving at night. You'd end up in a ditch, or worse."

"Then I'll accept the offer. Thanks."

RYAN TOLD HIS MOTHER and grandmother of his plans, and then went out and started both his and Susannah's trucks to warm them. He checked on Nia while Susannah said her goodbyes to the women.

Nia was still sulking, lying on her bed with tears on her sweet face and one arm around her favorite toy, a bear his mother had made from an old brown blanket.

Hell, he felt like a failure. All he wanted in life was to make this child happy, and he seemed incapable of it.

"I have to go out for a few minutes," he told her, sitting down. He stroked her hair. "Gran and Nana Sipsey will be here. Gran is making you something to eat, and then she's going to help you take a bath."

She didn't respond.

"I guess you're still mad at me, huh?"

She nodded.

"Too bad. I was hoping for a kiss. I haven't had one since this morning, and you know I can't go very long without some of that good Nia sugar."

She shook her head.

"No deal, huh? Okay, then." He started to rise, but she sat up, threw her arms around his neck and began to bawl.

"I'm sorry, Daddy. I didn't mean to be bad."

"I know you didn't, baby."

"Please don't give me away."

"Give you away? Sa Sa..." He untangled her arms, sat her in his lap and made her look at him. "Where did you get a crazy idea like that? I would *never* give you away."

"You'll love me for ever and ever?"

"Of course I will. Why would you think I'd give you away?"

"Because."

"Because why?"

"Just because."

He tried to coax her into talking, but she didn't seem to understand why she felt the way she did. Neither did he. He'd never given her any reason to believe she wasn't wanted. She was his life, his most important reason for existing.

"Baby, there's no need to worry. Daddy wouldn't do that. Not ever. No matter what."

"Promise?"

"I promise."

"If I was *really* bad?"

"Not even then. Listen to me, Nia. Nothing you could do would ever make me give you away or leave you. I love you too much. Do you understand?"

She said she did, and wiped her tears with the back of her hand.

"Good girl. Now stop crying. Everything's okay." Ryan took his handkerchief out of his pocket. "Let's blow that nose before it runs away." He held the cloth and she blew hard, making the honking sound that had led to her nickname. "That's my little goose."

"Cooper's nose is running, too."

"Uh-oh. We can't have that." He picked up the bear from the floor where he'd fallen and pretended to let him blow his nose. "Any other critters that need attention? No? Then, can I have a kiss?"

She gave him a big sloppy one.

"Where's Susannah?" she asked.

Oh, hell.

"She's downstairs saying goodbye to Gran and Nana Sipsey. She's about to leave."

"I want to."

"Want to what? Say goodbye?"

"Uh-huh."

"Do you promise to do it right this time and not make a fuss?"

"Uh-huh."

"Okay, then. Come on."

SUSANNAH TOOK the sack Ryan's mother handed her. "Thank you. I can't wait to taste it. I didn't know you could make jelly out of kudzu."

"We use only the blossoms, not the vine," Mrs. Whitepath told her. "Be sure and have Helen open a jar for your breakfast in the morning."

"I will."

Nana Sipsey also had a gift for her. She pressed a small cloth pouch into her hand.

"Med-cine," she said.

"Oh, thank you, but I already have medicine for my arm." The doctor had prescribed painkillers. She hadn't used them, though, the bottle was still full and tucked away in her makeup bag.

"No, no," the old woman said. She rattled off several words in Cherokee that Susannah didn't understand.

"Pardon?"

Mrs. Whitepath interpreted. "She says the medi-cine isn't for your arm, it's for your headache. Feverfew. It can taste bitter taken alone, so mix a few of the leaves in with your dinner tonight.''

"How did—?''

Ryan and Nia came into the kitchen then and Susannah never got the chance to ask how the old woman had known she had a headache. The pounding at her temples had started only a few minutes ago.

Nia ran over and immediately wanted Susannah to push up the sleeve of her sweater again. ''Is my name still there?''

''Right here.'' Susannah put down the jelly and showed the child. ''Having your name on my arm will be almost like having *you* with me wherever I go. We'll be together.''

Nia thought about that, and shook her head. ''Uh-uh, because I don't got your name anywhere.''

Bright kid.

''My goodness, you're absolutely right. How silly of me. Would you like me to write my name on something of yours?''

Her eyes lit up. ''Uh-huh.'' She turned to Ryan. ''Can she, Daddy?''

''Does she have an old T-shirt I could sign?'' Susannah asked Ryan.

''I think we can find something.''

''Cooper!'' Nia said, and ran off to get what Ryan explained was a stuffed toy.

When she returned, Susannah knelt and used a craft marker Mrs. Whitepath gave her to write her name on the shirt worn by Nia's teddy bear.

"There you go."

"Tell Susannah thank you," Ryan said.

"Thank you."

"You're welcome, Nia."

"Do you got to go away?"

"Yes, sweetheart, I do. I'm sorry."

"Can I kiss you goodbye?"

The request took Susannah off guard, but also touched her heart.

"Oh, I'd like that very much."

Nia clung to her after the kiss, and Ryan had to gently coax his daughter to let go. "Remember your promise, Sa Sa."

Once out the door, Ryan walked Susannah to the driver's door of her truck and helped her get in with her jelly.

"I appreciate your being so nice to Nia," he said.

"Being nice to her is easy. She's adorable. So sweet and loving."

"I know. Sometimes I can't believe how lucky I am to have her."

Susannah wanted to ask why he'd gotten custody instead of her mother, but she let the question slide. The subject was too personal. She didn't need to know, anyway. After tonight, she'd never see Ryan Whitepath or his family again.

The thought saddened her. She liked these people. For a few hours, she'd felt connected again, a part of something.

But maybe it was best that Ryan hadn't been able to take her on as a student. Caring about this family would be too easy, and she didn't ever want to care about anyone again. Love inevitably brought pain.

Some doors, she knew from experience, should be left closed and locked, especially those that led to the heart.

TEN MINUTES LATER, Ryan pulled his truck into the yard of Helen and Bascombe Miller. Susannah parked beside him.

Ryan had grown up with Bass and was as close to him as he was to his own brothers. Ryan also had high regard for Helen, who was eight months pregnant with their first child.

The couple was mixed race—he was Indian and she was white—and that had created a rift between Helen and her rich, upper-class parents.

He couldn't understand their reaction, but he was familiar with it. He'd been a victim of the same kind of prejudice when he'd left the mountain to go to school. Some people hadn't been able to see past his skin color.

"Thanks for doing this, Bass," Ryan told his friend while Helen helped Susannah settle in her room. "I didn't feel right letting her fend for herself."

"No problem."

Ryan followed him into the kitchen and poured himself a glass of tea from the pitcher in the fridge.

"Wait," Bass whispered. "I've got something to show you in the basement. My new toy."

In the dimly lit room below, Bass removed a long, thin case from behind a workbench cabinet and opened it. Inside was a new fishing rod. Bascombe loved fishing almost as much as he loved being a sheriff's deputy. He had more gadgets, rods, reels and tackle than anyone Ryan knew.

"Pure graphite with a custom-made Tennessee foregrip," Bass told him. He stroked the rod the way he would a favorite dog. "See the thread wraps on the guides? Tight. That's quality."

Ryan had to admit the workmanship was good. "How much?"

"Three twenty."

"Yow!"

"Yeah, expensive, but it's made to fit my hand."

"Let me know when you plan to tell Helen so I can go out of town that day."

"I thought I'd wait to mention it until after the baby comes and she doesn't feel so miserable."

"Smart move."

Bass put the fishing rod back in its hiding place. "So what's Susannah's story? How'd you meet her?"

"She's traveling around the country, and showed up at the house this afternoon wanting art lessons, but I'm busy right now with a couple of major contracts. I told her I couldn't do it."

"Too bad. She's a looker, or didn't you notice?"

"I noticed."

"Couldn't you find time?"

"Probably, but Nana's got this crazy idea that Susannah's been sent to help Nia, and the last thing I want to do is encourage that kind of thinking."

"I don't know, man. Your grandmother sensed before Helen did that she was pregnant."

"Yeah, but you were trying to have a baby. She made a lucky guess."

"What about old man Litton and the vision she had of him surrounded by flames? A month later his place was gone."

"He smoked like a chimney, Bass. I'm surprised he didn't burn the house down a long time ago."

"I'm just saying your grandmother's been right before and maybe you should put more stock in what she's telling you. Take a chance for once. Loosen up a little and stop thinking you have to be in control of everything."

"I can't afford to do anything that might hurt Nia. She's already formed an attachment to Susannah."

"I don't see what it would hurt for Nia to spend some time with her. Or you either, for that matter."

"It's a moot point. I've made my decision."

Helen yelled down the stairs, "What mischief is going on down there? I don't trust you two alone."

"Nothing's going on," Bass called out, and muttered to Ryan, "I'm still in the doghouse over that boat you talked me into bringing home."

"*I* talked you into? Hey, friend, spending eight thousand dollars on a used fishing boat without consulting your wife was *your* idea."

"I got a great deal! It was seventeen thousand new."

"Didn't I tell you she'd pitch a fit? You don't go out and buy a boat when your wife's getting ready to have a baby."

"She nearly didn't let me in the house. Hell, I still haven't made it back into the bed, not that there's much activity going on there right now, but it's the principle of the thing. A man should be king of his castle, you know?"

Ryan guffawed at that statement. "How would I know? I live with three females. Four if you count the cat. I'm the peon of my castle, not the king."

"She says we can't go off together again. You corrupt me."

His friend smiled broadly. *Bass* was the corrupter, and had been since they were both boys. Ryan had gotten in more trouble as a kid from following Bascombe than he cared to recall.

"I guess you told her it was my fault," Ryan said.

"Of course I did."

"Then I'm glad she's making you sleep alone."

Going back upstairs, they found the women putting plates on the table. Helen looked like she was about to whelp a whole litter rather than one baby and Ryan told her so. In the past week it seemed as if she'd gained twenty pounds.

"What a terrible thing to say to a woman three weeks from her due date." She pinched him playfully on the arm. "But I'll forgive you. Will you stay and eat supper with us?"

"I'd love to, but I need to get back and spend some time with Nia before she goes to bed."

"How's she doing?"

"About the same."

"I'm sorry. Why don't you come back when she's asleep and visit for a while? We haven't seen you in weeks."

"Can't. Got to work."

"That's all you do these days, Ryan."

"I know, but it's a busy time for me. Thanks for the invitation, but I'll do it some other night." He kissed her on the cheek. "See ya, Bass."

Susannah walked him to his truck. He got in and rolled down the window.

"It's been nice meeting you, Ryan."

"Same here. If I wasn't so bogged down—"

She waved away his apology over not being available to teach her. "Don't worry about it."

"Good luck with your list."

"My...?" She cringed with embarrassment. "I was hoping you hadn't read that stupid thing."

"Sorry. I saw part of it when I picked up the paper."

"You probably think it's silly."

"No, I don't."

"I wrote it because I don't want to look back on my life with regret. Now that I'm free of the responsibility of taking care of my mother, I want to try new things and go places I've never been before."

"I can understand that. Sometimes I wish I could start the truck, take off and drive wherever the road takes me."

"Exactly. I don't want to be tied down. I never again want to have to worry about anyone but myself."

"So your top item's what brought you here—your desire to create something that'll outlast you?"

"Yes."

"Sorry things didn't work out. I mean that, Susannah."

"I know."

He remembered some of the more personal items she'd included on her list and chuckled.

"What?" she asked.

"I was just thinking that having a shot at helping you out with number nine might've been a lot more interesting than number one."

"Number nine? What was that one?"

"I think," he said with a grin, "maybe I'd better let you look it up after I'm gone."

SUSANNAH RACED upstairs to her room when Ryan pulled out of the drive and went straight for her sketchbook.

She pulled out her Life List. Number nine read, "Wild uninhibited sex with a stranger."

"Oh, no!"

Dismay turned to amusement. She giggled and fell on the bed, laughing loudly.

Well, he was right. Working on number nine with the attractive Ryan Whitepath would have been very interesting indeed.

CHAPTER FIVE

NIA HAD ONE of her stomachaches, so Ryan put her to bed in her room at the barn, where he could work and still be close. According to the doctor, her pains were physical manifestations of the emotional pain she couldn't verbally express, but Ryan never discounted them. To Nia they felt real.

He read her an extra story and then another, staying until she felt better and went to sleep. The cat lay curled in her favorite spot at the foot of the bed. Ryan stroked Nia's dark head and kissed her, then scratched Abigail under the chin. He made sure the night-light was on, and he left the door open so he could hear if Nia stirred.

At two o'clock in the morning, a scream pierced the air. He was already up the stairs and at Nia's bedroom door when he heard the crash and the sound of breaking glass from inside. Abigail raced out as if being chased by hounds.

He flipped on the light. He found his daughter thrashing about, fighting some unknown demon in her sleep. She'd knocked over the lamp and the base lay in shards on the rug.

"Daddyyy!"

He scooped her up and held her against his chest. "I'm here, baby. Daddy's here."

Sobs racked her slender body. Her arms continued to flail.

"Wake up, Nia. You're having a bad dream."

"Daddy, help me!"

"Nia, wake up."

After a moment she pulled back and blinked at him with unfocused eyes. "Daddy?" Her voice remained pitiful, but at least she was starting to come around. She began to sob.

"I'm here, sweetheart. You're safe. It was only a bad dream."

"I'm scared."

"Of what?"

She said she didn't know. She couldn't remember what had frightened her in the dream.

He sat on the side of the bed and rocked her, but his efforts to calm her fears didn't seem to be doing any good. Her breathing was too heavy. She continued to cry and gasp for air until she hyperventilated, making the situation worse.

When her hands and feet started to go numb from too much oxygen, she thought she was dying and that scared her even more. Ryan took her to the bathroom, set her on the vanity and washed her face.

"You need to settle down, sweetheart. Stop crying and don't breathe so fast."

"I ca-n't," she said with a hitch in her voice.

"Yes, you can. Look at Daddy. Watch how I'm breathing." He took a couple of slow, shallow breaths. "See?"

"I ca-n't do it."

Without warning she vomited her dinner down the front of her pajamas. He helped her to the toilet, where she threw up a second time.

He washed her face again.

"That it?" he asked.

She nodded.

Ryan felt her brow and cheeks. She didn't seem feverish. She'd made herself sick from anxiety before, but never this bad.

He considered calling the rescue squad, or running her down to the emergency room in Andrews, but either one would take too long. She needed to calm herself and she needed to do it now. He did, too. His heart beat so hard he feared it might jump out of his chest.

He wasn't sure what to do.

"Baby, lie down on the floor. That's good." He wet the washcloth again, wrung it out and placed it on her forehead. "Close your eyes and try to think of something nice while Daddy calls Dr. Thompson.''

''Don't le-ave me.''

''I'm only going to get the phone. I'll be right back.''

He raced downstairs and grabbed the portable from his workbench. He dialed the doctor's emergency number on his way back to Nia. The doctor returned the call within a couple of minutes. Ryan explained the problem.

''Put Nia on the phone,'' she said.

Dr. Thompson was able to do what Ryan couldn't. Thankfully, Nia's breathing eased as they talked. She stopped crying and began to respond to the doctor's questions.

Ryan waited until he was satisfied she was all right. Then, while Nia was still speaking to the doctor, he slipped out to clean up the glass in her bedroom. He was trembling so badly he had to sit for a moment. He put his face in his hands and willed himself not to break down.

He didn't know how much more of this he could take. The worry, the frustration of not being able to help his child... His nerves were shot.

Nights were hell. He never slept well anymore, but drifted in and out, his ears trained to listen for any sound from her bedroom.

Days when he was able to coax her into going to

school, he worried about her being so far away. And the tension didn't leave during the days she was home. *Those* times he worried about her not being in school and falling behind in her class work. She was already in danger of having to repeat first grade.

He'd done everything he knew to do, but Nia wasn't getting better. If there was an answer to this problem, he had no idea where to find it.

Several minutes passed before he'd composed himself. He vacuumed the carpet, got a clean pajama top out of the drawer for Nia and returned to the bathroom, where she sat cross-legged on the floor mat. She actually tried to smile when he came in.

"She wants to talk to you, Daddy."

Ryan took the phone and put it in the crook of his neck so he could talk and remove Nia's soiled top at the same time.

"I think she'll be okay now," the doctor told him.

"I'm sorry I had to wake you. I didn't know what else to do."

"That's perfectly all right, Mr. Whitepath. That's why I'm here. Please call me back first thing in the morning so we can talk further. I'd like to know more about Nia's new friend."

"New friend?"

"Susannah."

RYAN HAD mixed feelings about his next conversation with Dr. Thompson. As arranged, they talked a second time at 6:00 a.m. Ryan explained the events of the day before, how Nia had come to know Susannah and how she'd responded to her.

"Interesting," the doctor said. "You might want to reconsider your decision not to give this woman lessons. For some reason, your daughter feels a connection to her, and that could be utilized. In the months I've been counseling Nia, this is the first time I've heard her animated about anything. She has a spark when she mentions Susannah."

"Which doesn't make sense to me. They were only together for a couple of hours. Nia's spent much more time with my sister, yet she hardly ever asks about Anita since she went back to school."

"Perhaps she identifies with Susannah because the woman also recently lost her mother. Her presence is comforting because here, finally, is someone who can understand how Nia feels. Or so Nia believes..."

Okay, Ryan conceded, but he relayed his concern about his daughter becoming too attached. "Couldn't she be hurt even more by Susannah leaving a second time?"

"That's certainly a risk, and I won't tell you she wouldn't be upset, but this could be a way to reinforce an important lesson. People Nia cares about are inevitably going to go out of her life. You have an elderly grandmother, for example, who in all likelihood will die before Nia reaches adulthood. If she can learn to appreciate the time she has with people rather than focusing on their departure, her life will be much more fulfilling.''

"I've tried to explain that already. And it's not like she hasn't lost people. She's had friends move away. And my brother and his wife moved out of town last year. That didn't seem to upset her.''

"I know, but her sole experience with *traumatic* separation has been her mother's death, and that was so sudden she never had time to prepare for the loss.''

True. Carla had died within twenty-four hours of his and Nia's arrival at her home in London. Her quick passing had been a shock even to him.

"If Nia understands from the outset that Susannah's stay is temporary,'' the doctor continued, "she has time to understand and accept it. It would also do her good to see someone else dealing with death and doing it appropriately. Do you believe this woman is stable?''

"I think so.''

"I hear reservation in your voice.''

He told her about Susannah selling her house, quitting her job and flitting around the country. "That's not something I'd do, but after learning she nursed her mother all those years, I can see where she'd want to cut her ties to the past and have a little adventure. What's your opinion?''

''I haven't met her, so it's difficult for me to render one, but her reaction is common. One of the steps of the grieving process is to suppress grief, to detach and distance ourselves from the trauma. You've seen that same behavior in Nia when she put away her mother's photograph and the dolls she gave her.''

''At least Susannah will talk about her mother. I try to get Nia to talk and she acts like Carla never existed.''

''Yet you say Nia had no problem speaking of her mother to Susannah.''

''No, apparently not.''

''Then having her spend a few weeks with Nia is an idea worth considering—if she's agreeable, of course, and if it wouldn't interfere with your work.''

''I'll give it some thought.''

And he did. He argued with himself until daylight, first about whether he should ask Susannah to stick around. He would, he decided. And second, about how much he should tell her. That decision was harder.

She'd made it clear she didn't want any entanglements. What was it she'd said? *I never again want to have to worry about anyone but myself.*

She might not stay if she understood the depth of

Nia's illness—or that *she* was the magic pill prescribed as part of the cure.

"So don't tell her," he mumbled to himself as he turned on the shower and prepared to make himself look more presentable. He'd dust off what little charm he had and offer her a deal she couldn't refuse.

He didn't like subterfuge. He'd been taught to be honest in his dealings with people and to respect them as he did his blood brothers and sisters. But after Nia's frightening episode last night, he was willing to try anything. Even lie to Susannah about the real reason he'd changed his mind about the job.

SUSANNAH WOKE early enough the next morning to watch the first rays of sunlight spread across the snow-covered trees. Standing in a robe on the private balcony outside her second-floor room, she breathed in the fresh air and experienced a rare moment of happiness.

If it was true that some places on earth were sacred, then these mountains were surely among them. She'd slept soundly for the first time in months. No nightmares. No waking up thinking she was back home and that her mother had cried out in the darkness.

Her good night's sleep might have been because of her exhaustion or the comfort of the wonderfully soft sheets and down pillows Helen had on the bed. The room was homey and comfortable and the quiet enveloped her like loving arms.

The "medicine" Ryan's grandmother had given her also played a part in her restful sleep. Assured by Bascombe that the leaves were harmless and would help her headache, Susannah had crumbled them in her dinner salad last night. Within ten minutes her pain had disappeared.

The crunch of footsteps below made her look down. Bass, dressed in his deputy's uniform and carrying a thermos, was walking his way to his truck.

"Morning," she called out.

He turned and looked up. "Morning. You're up early."

"Hard to sleep with views like this."

"That's what all our guests say. Helen's in the kitchen and I've already made coffee. Go get yourself a cup."

"Thanks, I will. And thanks for letting me stay last night, Bass. You have a lovely place."

"Anytime, Susannah. I hope you'll come back and see us again." He raised his hand in parting.

Susannah took a quick shower and laid out jeans and a long-sleeved red shirt.

Helen knocked gently. "Susannah?"

"I'm up." She slipped her robe back on and opened the door.

"Oh, good. I thought I heard the water running. Ryan's here. He wants to talk to you."

"Is something wrong? What did he say?"

"Only that he wanted to catch you before you left."

"Okay. Tell him I'll be right down."

She dressed quickly, ran a brush through her hair, and jogged downstairs to the kitchen, where Helen was cutting dough into biscuits on the counter. Ryan sat at the table with his hands around a steaming cup of coffee. He stood as she entered. He had a haggard look and dark circles under his eyes.

"Is your family okay?" she asked.

"Can we talk a minute?"

"Nia?"

"She's fine. My mother's getting her ready for school."

"You don't look well, Ryan. Are you okay?"

He ran a hand through his loose hair. "I haven't been to bed yet. I worked all night."

"That can't be good for you."

"Actually that's why I'm here." He glanced at Helen. "Do you mind if Susannah and I talk in the den?"

"Of course not. I'll make you both some breakfast."

"Thanks, Helen," he said, "but none for me."

Susannah poured herself a cup of coffee and they

walked to the den with its rustic beams and rough wood walls. The house was more like a lodge—four bedrooms and a private bath for each on the second floor, plus several large rooms downstairs for eating and entertaining. Helen and Bass had their own bedroom, bath and small sitting room off the kitchen.

A fire burned in the massive stone fireplace. Susannah took a seat on the leather couch in front of it. Ryan preferred a chair.

"What's up?" she asked.

"I've been giving a lot of thought to what you said yesterday about how learning the computer would save me time. I want to take you up on your offer to help. In exchange, I'll give you the mosaic lessons you want, let you work with me on a project or two and also pay you a salary. You can live in the cabin across from the workshop while you're here. My interns have found it comfortable."

Susannah didn't know how to respond.

"Interested?" he asked.

"Why the sudden turnabout?"

"Like you said, I need to get better organized. I've been thinking about trying again to hire someone to handle bills and deal with customer calls. You're a nice person and apparently competent. I doubt you'll drive me crazy like the last woman. It's a plus that you also have artistic talent. And that my family likes you."

"I like them, too."

"So you'll do it?"

"You understand I could only stay here for about eight weeks. Until Christmas, or a few days before it. I want to be in New York for New Year's Eve."

"That's fine."

"Does your family observe Christmas? It didn't occur to me until this moment that you might not."

"We do, but more traditionally than most people. Our celebration also involves the Winter Solstice, which falls on December 22. We decorate, burn a Yule log, light fires and say prayers to bring back the sun. Our gifts are made by hand rather than purchased."

"That sounds lovely. I wouldn't be an intrusion to your holiday plans if I stay?"

"No, not at all."

"I wish I had more time to offer you, but I don't."

"A few weeks will be enough. You can get me started on the computer and help clean up the files. Maybe we could spend a couple of hours every morning. After that, I'll teach you about mosaics as we tackle some projects. You can help me with a mural I'm doing for the community center here and knock number one off your list."

"You'd trust me with that?"

"You can follow instructions and a pattern, can't you?"

"Yes."

"Then I trust you. How's five hundred dollars a week sound?"

"Too generous for what you're expecting. You wouldn't have to pay me. I'm thrilled to simply be able to work with you."

"No, I insist. You'll be putting in a lot of hours and you deserve a salary."

"But you'd already be giving me lessons *and* a place to live. That's enough."

"If I hired you or anyone else with your experience as my permanent office manager, I'd have to shell out a lot more than that."

"True."

"Then it's settled."

"Not quite. One more thing." She was embarrassed to bring this up, but felt she needed to clear the air. "So there won't be any misunderstandings between us…I'm really not looking for a relationship, even a temporary one." Heat crept up her neck. "Just because I put something on my list doesn't mean I'm actively seeking to do it right now. Do you get my meaning?"

He smiled, amused. "You mean we can't do number nine? Well, hell."

"Don't tease me, Ryan. I'm mortified enough as it is."

"I can't help it. Your face is redder than your shirt."

"I just don't want you to think... Not that you aren't attractive, because you are, but..." She rolled her eyes. Oh, good Lord! Had she really said that out loud? "You know what I mean. This has to be a business arrangement."

"Don't worry, Susannah," he told her with a chuckle. "I'm only offering a job."

"Sorry. I had to make sure."

"You have to negotiate separately for sex."

She tried not to blush any more than she already had, but didn't succeed. "You really enjoy making me squirm, don't you?"

"Yeah."

"Can we please just get back to business?"

"All right," he said, nodding, but he didn't stop smiling. "Let's settle this. If you accept my offer I only have one condition. You have to stay the whole two months. Until December twenty-third, let's say. You can't up and leave if you get bored and decide there's someplace else you'd rather be."

"I wouldn't do that. I'd honor my commitment."

"I'd want your word. I can't rearrange my work schedule only to have you run out on me."

"That's reasonable."

"Then let's give it a go."

She still had some reservations. His change of heart seemed a bit odd, given how adamant he'd been last night. But she'd be getting to train with someone whose work she admired *and* getting money for it, which she could use.

"Sounds great," she told him. "When do we start?"

AFTER HE RETURNED home and had taken Nia to the bus, Ryan's next stop should have been bed, but he had one more thing he needed to do before getting some sleep.

He parked at the barn and walked to the house. Thankfully, he could see Nana Sipsey in her workroom checking her dried herbs, so he didn't have to face her again right now. He couldn't stand another one of her gleeful, I-told-you-so looks.

"Etsi?" he called out. He found his mother folding clothes in the laundry off the kitchen. He said he was headed up the mountain for a little while.

"Halayv dvhilutsi?" she asked. *When will you return?*

"In a couple of hours."

She nodded, but didn't say anything more, and Ryan sighed. He couldn't understand why she was upset with him.

"I thought you'd be as happy as Nana that I asked

Susannah to stay. You're the one who believes in Nana's prophesy mumbo jumbo, not me.''

"I *am* happy. I like Susannah very much. But your dishonesty disturbs me. She's a nice woman and you should have told her the truth.''

"She never would've agreed to stay if I had.''

"You have no faith in people, son. And for someone who embraces his heritage as strongly as you do, you turn a blind eye to our teachings rather a lot—whenever it suits you, in fact.''

"Meaning?''

"We are all part of something larger than ourselves. These connections—one thing to another, one person to another, spirit world to physical world—support us. Alone, the flower couldn't reproduce so *Elohi* has made the bee to carry the pollen from plant to plant. The tree drops its branches and the bird uses the twigs to build its nest. Surprising, isn't it, how when something is needed, it's given?''

"What does this have to do with Susannah?''

"You've been sent a gift, perhaps the very thing you need for Nia, and yet you don't accept it as offered. You still try to manipulate and control it.''

"Because I have a responsibility to my daughter and her welfare.''

"Yes, but sometimes you forget you are not alone in your responsibility—and not only to your child.''

"You're not making sense."

"When your father left, you stepped in and helped take care of all of us, even though you were only a boy. You've continued to do that, sending Charlie and Anita to school, helping Joseph start his carpentry business, providing for me and your grandmother. We all appreciate what you've done. But I worry about the heavy burden you carry, even more so since Nia was born."

"I don't mind that, and you know it. I've got the money."

"It's not the financial burden, but the emotional one you must share, along with yourself."

"Myself? Huh?"

She pinched his ear, as she used to do when he was little and being thick-headed. "You've grown into a fine man, but you still have much to learn."

THE CAVE where his ancestors had hidden from the soldiers back in the 1830s was a forty-five minute hike through difficult terrain, but Ryan could follow the trail in the dark if he had to.

Branches, small rocks and boards hid the secret entrance and prevented bears and other creatures from using it. Years ago he'd covered a hole in the rocks above with heavy wire mesh. The grate kept out bats, but still allowed the rising smoke from campfires within the cave to disperse.

You could smell a fire if you were close enough, but the smoke mingled with the blue haze this far up and wasn't detectable by sight.

His ancestors had been blessed with good fortune. The cave, the abundance of natural resources and the inaccessibility from the outside world, had allowed *Numma hi tsune ga* and his parents to avoid capture until the government granted amnesty to them and the others who'd held out against relocation.

Ryan moved aside the obstruction and crawled in. Three feet beyond the opening, the tunnel opened out and became a room, the larger of two. He stood and brushed the dirt and snow from his clothes. Using the flashlight he'd brought, he found his supplies and the oil lantern and matches he kept among them.

As a boy he'd camped out here hundreds of times, even staying overnight, and strangely he'd never been affected by the isolation or the sounds of the creatures who moved about in the night.

This place gave him peace. He came here when he sought answers or his problems seemed unbearable.

He struck a match and the lantern came to life, illuminating his favorite part of the cave—the walls—decorated by the former inhabitants with crude pictures of animals and their own handprints.

His grandfather, upon purchasing the land, had

added his handprint and identified it with his Indian name. Ryan's father's was to the right of it, painted when he was still a young boy.

At nine, Ryan had placed his own hand against the wall and written his name, *Siquuitsets,* possum, underneath.

His siblings, as was now tradition, had added theirs when they'd been old enough to understand the significance of it.

He removed his jacket and shirt. He drew a large circle in the dirt and in the center of it built a fire to say prayers to The Great One and to the seven sacred directions, using sycamore wood for east, beech for south, oak for west, birch for north, pine for center, locust for above and hickory for below.

His grandmother had taught him how to find and grind the red paint. Putting some in a wooden bowl, he mixed it with water from the trickling drops of melted snow that had collected in a rock depression. He smeared lines down his face and across his naked chest. He lit the fire and stood before it.

"To the Fire Spirit in the East,

"To the Earth Spirit in the South,

"To the Water Spirit in the West,

"To the Wind Sprit in the North,

"To Elohi, Mother Earth,

"To Galunlati, the Above World,

"To Adanvdo, the Center that connects all things,

"To Ogedoda, The Great One and creator,

"I give thanks for your wisdom and your patience.

"I humbly ask forgiveness for any hurt I've caused any living thing.

"I honor those who came before me, those who are with me and those who will come after me.

"Hear me, Ogedoda. I seek your healing power for my daughter. Guide me in my decisions so that she may grow up strong in body and mind. Show me the path to knowledge and understanding.

"May the smoke carry my prayers to you."

He watched as it curled upward, went through the hole and journeyed toward the sky.

"And so it is good."

CHAPTER SIX

THE CABIN WAS ONE rectangular room with a tiny adjoining bathroom, but Susannah liked the old iron bed. The other furniture was either handmade or high-quality reproductions.

A covered porch ran the length of the building. The back door stood directly opposite the front and a colorful floor runner stretched between them. That divided the space into halves.

A couple of chairs and a table big enough for eating or working on her computer occupied the kitchen. A door on that side led to the bathroom.

On the left was a stone fireplace, the double bed, a couch with cushions covered in a striped Indian print, a small trunk that served as a coffee table and a waist-high bookcase holding several local guidebooks and assorted paperbacks. The last resident had obviously been a hiker and mystery-novel reader.

Large picture windows set in both the front and back walls made her feel as if she were outside. She could look out the rear window or door and see the mountain with the house nestled at one edge of the clearing.

Ryan's place sat about a hundred yards away to the right, on the other side of the driveway leading to the house.

From the front window she had the same awe-inspiring view she'd admired last evening from Mrs. Whitepath's steps.

She puzzled over the position of the claw-footed tub in the kitchen until Ryan's mother showed up and explained.

"My husband built us this place thirty-one years ago when we got married so we could be away from his parents. He called it our honeymoon cabin. I loved it except for one thing. Ned only installed a shower, which wouldn't do. I like my baths."

"Same here."

"I cajoled, whined and begged for a bathtub until he finally gave in, but the bathroom didn't have space, even for a small one. Hence, it wound up out here. The pleasure you'll get from using it, though, is worth its unusual location."

"I'll bet it is." The thing was huge. Susannah couldn't wait to fill it up and soak. "Who made the furniture?"

"Ned and his father. They built the cabinets, too. I've had the couch reupholstered a few times since then, but the rest is original."

"Everything's lovely."

"Unfortunately, I didn't get to enjoy it very long. When I got pregnant with Ryan, moving to the house with Nana Sipsey and Papa George seemed the practical thing to do since they had plenty of room, but I came to miss this little place." She looked about wistfully. "Ned and I had some good times here."

"Are you sure you don't mind me using it? I could make other arrangements."

"No, I'm happy to have you." She handed Susannah towels and clean linens for the bed, then drew her finger across the table. "The furniture could use a bit of dusting, I'm afraid. I haven't cleaned in here in a while."

"That's okay. I'll take care of it."

"Ryan called Joe, my youngest boy, to come over and turn the water back on—he's handy with things like that. He also checked the chimney and water heater to make sure everything's working as it should."

"I appreciate that."

"Joe said he'd bring you some more wood when he got a chance, although there seems to be enough in the woodpile for a week or so. You have electric heat, too." She motioned to a wall heater that was blasting hot air. "You might prefer to use that all the time and forget about struggling with the fireplace. I always found it inconvenient. Light it or not—that's up to you. If you do use it, just be careful about going off and leaving the fire unattended."

"Okay."

"There's no phone, but you're welcome to use mine whenever you need."

"Ryan's already offered me his."

"Would you like me to bring down a small television? There's one in Anita's room you could have."

"Don't bother. I have a CD player I like listening to. Even when I have a TV in the room, I rarely turn it on."

She helped Susannah make the bed, then got blankets out of a built-in storage cabinet. On the table she placed a bouquet of dried flowers in a vase, a present from Ryan's grandmother.

"I'll leave you alone now so you can settle in. Ryan's trying to catch a couple of hours' sleep, but I'm sure he'll be over shortly. Let me know if you need anything else."

"You've been wonderful, Mrs. Whitepath. Your whole family has."

"I'd be delighted if you'd call me Annie. And Ryan's grandmother is Nana Sipsey—Nana to everyone."

"Thank you, Annie. And please thank Nana Sipsey for the flowers."

After Annie left, Susannah set about moving in. She had few possessions, but that was fine because there wasn't much space, anyway.

The small closet had a hanging rod and a couple of shelves and was adequate for what she owned—a jacket, one summer and one winter dress with matching shoes and a few casual outfits. For ease, she'd kept her wardrobe to a minimum.

The only personal articles she'd held on to were the family photo albums and her mother's jewelry.

She dusted the furniture and put her albums on the trunk. Her chores finished, she stepped back and looked around.

For the first time, she felt a longing for the things she'd given up when she sold the house, even those she'd never imagined she'd miss—like the grandfather clock that sat in the hallway for more than twenty-five years and annoyingly chimed on the quarter hour.

That sound, she realized now, had provided comfort to her when she was growing up. She missed it.

She missed the ugly lamps, too, the ones with peonies on them that her mother had found for a dollar a piece at a yard sale years ago and insisted on putting in the living room. She missed that awful dressing table with its frilly skirt trimmed in white eyelet. And the tea pitcher that, despite its hairline crack, had never leaked a drop and sat on the table at nearly every meal.

The cabin was charming, but it belonged to someone else and was decorated with someone else's things.

Be content with that, Susannah.

She had to remind herself that her life was different now. The people she'd loved were lost to her by one means or another. And no place would ever feel like home again.

"SHE'S REALLY, really gonna live with us?" Nia asked Ryan, her face showing her excitement.

He'd driven into Robbinsville and picked her up from school instead of letting her ride the bus. He figured he needed the quiet time alone with her to explain the situation, why Susannah was suddenly around again.

"Not *live* with us. For a few weeks, Susannah will be staying in the cabin and helping me with my work. Do you remember Brian with the long beard who stayed there two summers ago? He used to tease and tell you his name was Booger."

"Uh-uh." She shook her head.

"I guess you were too little. How about when Uncle Charlie and Aunt Barbara moved to the city and they stayed in the cabin for a couple of weeks until their new place was ready?"

"Aunt Barbara let me put pictures on the 'frigerator."

"That's right. She did. This'll be sort of the same. Susannah will stay in the cabin but only for a little while. Then she'll be going away."

"Where?"

"To New York."

"Where's that?"

"We'll get out the atlas tonight and I'll show you."

He parked the truck at the barn and told Nia to go in and hang up her backpack. "We'll say hello to Susannah before we look up your word definitions."

"Are we staying here tonight, Daddy, or with Gran and Nana?"

Shuttling back and forth between their place and his mother's and having two bedrooms got to be confusing for her at times.

"We're *home* tonight."

Nia hung her backpack and jacket in the kitchen, while Ryan went through the mail and put away the groceries he'd bought in town. He took a minute to slip a couple of steaks into marinade and pat out a hamburger to cook for Nia.

She insisted on taking time to draw a picture for Susannah with her crayons. Afterward, the two of them walked over to the cabin. Nia kept running ahead and Ryan had to keep ordering her to slow down. That part of the drive still had a few icy spots.

They found Susannah sitting on the porch, enjoying the day's pleasant weather. Their arrival frightened the snowbirds pecking for seeds beneath the melting snow. The creatures scattered with a flurry of wings.

Nia threw herself excitedly into Susannah's arms.

"Hey, be careful," Ryan warned her. "Remember her wrist."

"Sorry."

"That's okay," Susannah told her. "You didn't hurt me."

"I made you a present."

"You did?" She beamed a smile. "Let me see." Nia showed her the drawing with its crude house and stick people, and from Susannah's reaction, you would've thought his daughter was Picasso. "You made this? I can't believe how talented you are. Why, you draw as well as your daddy."

She winked at Ryan over the top of Nia's head and he felt a tightening where he shouldn't.

Too pretty, all right. Too nice. Too damn sexy. He was going to have a hell of a time behaving himself.

"The picture's for your 'frigerator," Nia told her.

"Let's go put it up."

Nia went ahead, with Susannah a few steps behind. Ryan followed them in.

"Do you have everything you need?" he asked Susannah, looking around.

"Yes, thanks. Your mother helped me."

"Did she warn you not to put any garbage outside?"

"No, she didn't mention that."

"Separate the recyclables, if you don't mind—glass, paper, aluminum—and put any vegetable-based waste in a bucket to throw in Nana's compost bin. And when you have a bagful of garbage, let me know and I'll take care of it. I don't want you scared by some four-footed visitor scrounging for meat scraps in the middle of the night."

"Uh, neither do I."

"I'll bring you some containers."

She told him again how much she appreciated his letting her use the cabin and said she was ready to start her job.

"Tomorrow's soon enough," he told her. "Or we can wait until Monday, since tomorrow's Friday."

"I'd rather get started immediately."

"Okay. That's fine."

"What time?"

"I take Nia to the bus stop every morning, but I'm back by eight. Walk over anytime after that."

"What's your schedule?"

"I work whenever I can get a minute, but you should plan on helping weekdays from around eight to three with a break for lunch. I leave again at three-thirty to pick up Nia and we're home by four except on Tuesdays, when she has ballet down at the community center. She's in bed and usually asleep by eight on school nights. I go back to the studio after that."

Every second Monday he also took her to her therapist after school, but her next appointment wasn't for a week. This information was best left unsaid, for the moment anyway.

"Do you work weekends?"

"Saturdays."

"And how often do you try to kill yourself working all night?" Susannah asked.

"Not often. Last night was an exception." Sleep had eluded him after Nia's episode. He'd simply put the time to good use.

"Don't hesitate to let me know how I can help, Ryan. I can run errands and get supplies. I could even take Nia to catch the bus and pick her up, if it'll save you time."

He almost confessed his deceit then. Obviously she liked Nia and didn't mind being with her. Maybe she wouldn't care that he'd hired her only to befriend his daughter.

"Thanks," he told her instead. With Nia there,

now wasn't the time to be making such revelations. "I'm sure we'll find plenty for you to do."

She got some tape so Nia could attach her drawing and commented on what a lovely present it was.

"I can make you more," Nia told her. "I draw flowers real pretty, don't I, Daddy?"

"She's an A-Number-One flower artist," Ryan agreed.

"Then flowers it is," Susannah told her. "I could use some pictures in here."

"Do you got crayons?"

"Mm, afraid not. Maybe you can draw it for me at your house and bring it over the next time you come. Would that be okay?"

Nia agreed it would.

"Well, we'd better go," Ryan told her.

"You just got here."

"I know, but Nia has homework, and I like to get that out of the way. We also need to spend a few minutes with Mom and Nana." He hesitated, hoping he wasn't about to make a fool of himself. "How about joining Nia and me for supper? I picked up steaks to grill."

"You don't eat at your mother's?"

"Some nights, but not tonight. I already told her not to expect us and that I was going to ask you over."

"Oh? Well, then I'd love to come. I haven't had

a chance to buy any supplies yet. All I have is a pack of peanut-butter crackers. Steak sounds much better. But are you sure? I wouldn't want to intrude on your time with Nia.''

"You won't. We'd enjoy the company. Wouldn't we, Sa Sa?"

Nia jumped up and down and begged her to say yes. "I can show you Dora, Boo and Jessie."

"Are those kittens?"

Nia giggled. "No, they're my babies."

Ryan explained that they were dolls associated with her favorite TV shows and movies.

"Ah…babies. I see. Okay, but I don't change diapers, young lady, especially stinky ones."

Nia fell into a new fit of giggles.

Ryan couldn't help chuckling himself. A weight seemed to lift from his shoulders. He'd done the right thing in asking Susannah to stay. She was going to be good for Nia.

"We won't ask you to do any diaper-changing," he told her, "but we might put you to work making a salad."

"Vegetables I can handle. No problem."

"Then we'll expect you about six. I'll leave the door unlocked."

SHE NEEDED new clothes. Her "best" jeans had somehow acquired a hole in the knee. The back pocket was coming off the only other clean pair she had.

Sighing, Susannah decided the second pair, although more faded, would have to do. With a sweater, maybe the rip wouldn't be noticeable.

After a long bath, she covered the freckles on her nose as well as she could with makeup, and applied a hint of mascara and lipstick. A quick brush through her hair to give it shine and she was ready to go.

Once at the barn, she let herself in the door. The kitchen and den of Ryan's living area were at the rear of the loft. Glass walls made those rooms visible from below. The drapes were drawn back and she could see Ryan puttering around in the kitchen; Nia sat at the counter watching him.

Abigail approached her on the stairs, wearing a dress and an old-fashioned granny cap tied under her neck. Unhappy about it, she swished her tail.

"Oh, dear, what happened to you?"

The cat mewed pitifully in response.

Susannah entered the door to the den and called out a greeting. Ryan waved her in. "Perfect timing," he announced.

Nia met her with a hug and the present of another drawing. Susannah took off her jacket, tossing it over a chair.

"Does your cat have a date? She looks pretty snazzy."

"What?" Ryan asked.

"The cat has a dress and hat on."

"Nia," Ryan said, giving her a stern look, "what did I tell you about putting your doll clothes on Abigail?"

"I forgot."

"No, you didn't forget. You just ignored what I said."

"But, Daddy, we were having a tea party and you can't go to a tea party without clothes on."

"What did I say about dressing the cat?"

"That she could get tangled up and hurt."

"That's right. And you wouldn't want to do anything to hurt her, would you?"

"Uh-uh. I love Abigail."

"Then go take them off. And if you *forget* again, no watching Powerpuff Girls for a week."

She looked like she was going to sulk for being scolded. Not wanting a repeat of last night's temper tantrum, Susannah jumped in. "Come on, I'll help you and then you can show me your room. I'm anxious to meet your babies." To Ryan she said, "Can you do without me for a few minutes?"

"Go ahead. I'm not ready to put the steaks on yet."

They freed poor Abigail from her outfit. Still

miffed, she streaked away and disappeared out the pet door.

Once in Nia's room, Susannah sat on the bed with Nia next to her and was introduced to each doll and stuffed animal. The child had dozens of toys.

"But Cooper's my favorite," she said, hugging the bear. "He's not a real bear. He only looks like one."

"Is that so? I'm glad to know that."

"Real bears are scary. They eat people. We have bears out there in the woods so you better be careful."

"Oh, I will. Thanks for warning me."

"Daddy says you're going to New Ork. He showed me on the map. He says I've been there before but I don't remember."

"It's called New *York*. They have interesting things I've always wanted to see."

"We have int'resting things. Last summer Daddy and Uncle Bass took me out in a boat and I had to be real quiet. Uncle Bass said 'damn' when the fish ate the food. That's a bad word."

"Oops, it sure is."

"I'm not supposed to say that, but it's okay 'cause I'm only telling you what Uncle Bass said."

"I think this one time it's all right."

"Uncle Bass isn't my real uncle, but Daddy says

to call him that 'cause he's like a real uncle. Him and Aunt Helen.''

"I met them. They're very nice.''

"I liked riding in a boat, but it don't got a place for little girls to tee tee.''

Susannah's lips twitched. She tried not to laugh. "I can see that would be a problem.''

"If you don't go away, maybe Daddy and Uncle Bass will give us a ride.''

"That sounds like fun, but I can't stay. I'm only going to be here a few weeks.''

"When are you going away?''

"Around Christmas.''

"Do you got to?'' Her face was so solemn, Susannah felt bad for making her unhappy.

"I'm afraid I do.'' Her instincts warned her to be careful. She could easily break this child's heart— or her own—if she foolishly allowed herself to get too close. "Friends sometimes have to go away, Nia. But we can have a good time while I'm here. We can draw and play with your dolls.''

"Can we bake brownies?''

"I guess we could. I'll ask about that.''

"I like the gooey ones with nuts.''

"Yum, me too.'' She patted her leg. "No need to be sad. We'll have lots of fun. Now, come on. Your daddy's going to wonder what happened to us.''

THE STEAKS were delicious. After dinner they played two quick games of Chinese checkers with

Nia. Susannah loaded the dishwasher while Ryan supervised Nia's bath and put her to bed.

Susannah said a quick good-night to the child. She left father and daughter picking out a story to read.

Ryan returned to the kitchen ten minutes later. "I told you I'd clean up."

"I didn't mind. Nia asleep?"

"Yeah, she dropped off by the time I got to the third page."

"Poor kid. She could hardly keep her eyes open during the game. She fought and fought to stay awake."

"She didn't sleep well last night. Nightmares."

"Does that happen often?"

"Occasionally."

"I guess that's one thing that never changes. I used to dream about road machinery chasing me when I was little. Cranes. Big dump trucks. That sort of thing. What about you? What did you find scary?"

"The usual stuff. Monsters. Falling. Going to school without my clothes on."

"I've dreamed about the last one," she said, smiling. "What about forgetting the combination to your locker?"

"Oh, yeah. And not knowing you were having a test until you got to class."

"Funny how universal nightmares are."

"I didn't really have that much of a problem with them. Charlie did, though. He had a thing about chickens."

"Chickens?" She wiped her hands on the dish-towel and hung it on the rack. "What's scary about chickens?"

"My great-uncle, Nana's brother, had a henhouse. To keep me from stealing the eggs, he said the hens would peck me to death if I got near them. At first, I didn't believe it. I was ten and thought I was pretty hot stuff. But I wasn't taking any chances. I paid Charlie to go in to see if they'd attack him. He was five and you could get him to do anything if you gave him a penny."

"You used your little brother as bait?"

"In those days, I thought that's all they were good for. But the plan backfired. One of the hens flew near his face and scared him. He fell down and started screaming bloody murder and sent all the birds into a panic. When Nana Sipsey found out what I'd done, she took a switch to my backside and blistered it good. And she blistered Charlie's be-cause he was gullible enough to listen to me."

"You're too funny."

"He still hasn't forgiven me. He had bad dreams for years about killer chickens."

"I don't blame him."

He got a bag of coffee out of the refrigerator and started to measure some into the drip machine on the counter.

"Can I interest you in a cup?" he asked.

"No, none for me. I should be going anyway and let you get back to work."

"Don't rush off. Talk to me while this brews."

"Okay, for a few minutes."

She took a stool at the island separating the kitchen from the den. When Ryan remained standing on the other side, she said a silent prayer of thanks. Her body was doing crazy things tonight, reacting to his smell, his voice. The farther away he stayed, the better.

The dark-green shirt seemed tailor-made to fit his broad shoulders. The tan corduroys showed off his flat stomach and narrow hips.

Had he dressed up for her? The thought made her a bit breathless.

"What will we work on tomorrow?" she asked, trying to keep her mind—and gaze—directed toward something safer than Ryan Whitepath's splendid body. "What mosaics are priority?"

"The tile repairs for a mosque ceiling in California. Very detailed. Very old. The new pieces have to be aged to match perfectly or they'll stand out.''

"Sounds interesting. And what's the community center project you said I could help you with?"

"We'll run over there sometime tomorrow and you can see where it's going. I've completed the majority of the panels, but there's still a couple more, plus grouting. If Helen doesn't screw me up with her delivery, we should have that finished in time for the Christmas opening."

"What's Helen got to do with it?"

"The mural has caricatures of the people of Sitting Dog. I want to include the baby in a pink or blue blanket, but Helen doesn't want to know the sex until it's born."

"Neither would I."

"Bass is also reluctant to put up an image representative of the baby before its birth. He's afraid we'd be asking for trouble."

"That's a bit odd, isn't it?"

"What can I say?" Ryan grinned. "He's superstitious."

"Are you the same way?"

"Yeah, I guess I am to some extent. I've been brought up to believe in good spirits and bad ones and not to tempt the bad ones."

"Angels and demons?"

"You could call them that. My mother is Christian but my grandmother, although she goes to church with us, holds fast to the old ways of our tribe. They brought me up to be open to the beliefs of each and my faith is an amalgamation of what they've both taught me. I believe in what some call God, but I know Him by another name. My understanding of creation, temptation, the flood, paradise...probably isn't very different from yours, only it has a *Tsalagi* twist to it.''

"I suppose my faith is all that kept me going during my mother's illness, but I have to admit it also wavered at times. I found it difficult to understand why *her.* I guess everyone who's ever had a relative die feels like that. Life isn't fair. Death has no rules.''

"Some things are beyond our ability to comprehend. Carla was only twenty-nine when she died and she'd been a fanatic about taking care of herself. Exercised every day. Ate right. Her job was stressful, I guess, but in a good way. She loved it. She was the last person I'd ever have imagined would die from disease.''

"What kind of work did she do?''

"She was in acquisitions and appraisals for Christie's London auction house. Her specialty was Art Deco jewelry.''

"What a great job. She must've been very smart.''

"She was. And a nice person. We just weren't right for each other."

"I know how that is. I've had experience with it myself. How did you meet her?"

"On the way home after finishing my graduate work, I stopped in London to catch an auction of Impressionist paintings, not that I could afford any of them, but some hadn't been available for public viewing in decades. Carla offered to show me around the city and I ended up extending my stay by two weeks. I'd been home a month when she called and said she was pregnant."

The coffee stopped dripping. He poured himself a cup. "I guess you've been wondering why Nia lives with me."

"Well…yes, but it's not that unusual these days for a father to raise a child."

"Carla didn't want children. She'd worked hard to establish herself in a tough field. Luckily for me, she was willing to sign over full custody."

"Did Nia visit?"

"Once a year. They weren't close, though. Carla really never had time for her and Nia sensed it, but she still feels a loss now that her mother's gone."

"Nia must take after her mother in appearance."

"Yeah, Carla wasn't what you'd call beautiful, but she was an attractive woman and Nia resembles her. I see it more and more every day. She inherited her mother's light skin and brown eyes.''

He looked toward the doorway and cocked his head, listening.

She turned around and looked, too, but didn't see anything. ''Something wrong?'' she asked.

''I thought I heard Nia.'' They were both quiet for a moment. ''Probably my imagination but let me go check on her. Be right back.''

He returned a minute later, saying she was still asleep.

Susannah glanced at her watch. Eight-thirty. ''I should go. If you don't get back to work, you'll be up too late, and I don't want a crabby boss tomorrow.''

''Me, crabby?'' he teased. ''Never.'' He put down his cup. ''I'll walk you to the door.''

They reached it, and she felt awkward saying good-night. Her attraction to him had caught her by surprise.

''Thanks for dinner. I enjoyed it.''

''Me, too, Susannah. Thanks for coming.''

He helped her put on her jacket. The collar got turned under and he straightened it, his fingers lingering a bit longer than necessary. His touch, even through the heavy fabric, had the same effect as if he'd caressed her bare skin. She had to force herself to be still and not jump away.

"See you in the morning," she said.

"Lock your doors. And remember what I said about the trash."

"I will."

He watched until she went inside the back door of the cabin. She waved, indicating she was safe, and then did what he'd said and bolted everything up tight.

As she crawled into bed later, she admitted that he was right. Danger existed for her here—but not from nocturnal animals. Ryan Whitepath was interesting and sexy. His daughter took first prize as the most adorable kid on the planet.

"Damn," she said out loud with a groan. What the hell had she gotten herself into?

CHAPTER SEVEN

SUSANNAH ARRIVED for work the next morning shortly after Ryan got back from putting Nia on the bus. He figured she must've been watching for him out her window.

"Hey," she said, yawning.

"Hey, sleepyhead. I picked up biscuits if you're hungry. There's also coffee."

"Coffee would be great." She opened the lid on one of the foam cups and took a sip. "Mmm, that's good."

Her hair was still a bit tousled and she hadn't tried to hide the splattering of freckles across the bridge of her nose as she'd done last night. Some women, like Carla, improved with makeup. This one had an appealing earthiness, a natural beauty that didn't need it.

"How'd you sleep?" he asked.

"Like a log. I zonked out immediately. I had a terrible time waking up."

"The mountain air will do that to you."

"I guess that was it."

"Hopefully it wasn't the after-dinner conversation."

"Don't be silly. I had a great time."

"I was afraid I bored you talking about Carla."

"No, I'm glad you told me. Knowing helps me understand Nia better. I wouldn't want to do or say anything out of ignorance that might make her grief worse."

"I appreciate that, Susannah. She could use a friend right now."

"How *was* she this morning?"

"Good."

"Any bad dreams?"

"No, she slept okay."

She'd wet her bed, something she hadn't done in a while, but Ryan wasn't too concerned about it.

He emptied cream and two sugars into his coffee and stirred it. "Last night you said you understood about people not being compatible. You looked sad. Were you speaking from experience?"

"That's a big question to ask me so early in the morning."

"Hey, I told you my story. It's only fair you tell me yours."

"There's not much to tell. I was engaged. He dumped me."

"Who was he?"

"An attorney."

"One of your bosses?"

"Heavens, I wasn't that crazy." She yawned again. "He worked for another firm."

"What happened? Why did the relationship go sour?"

"He couldn't cope with my family responsibilities. Mother was in the late stages of her disease at the time. He broke it off and asked me to give back his ring."

"Jerk."

"I'd argue, but you're right. I'm at least thankful he realized he didn't want to marry me *before* we walked down the aisle."

"Is he one of the reasons you decided to hit the road?"

"I guess he was part of it. I needed a change in my life. Everything around me was a reminder of the sickness and heartache the past several years had brought me. I also regretted that I'd never done anything important or exciting."

"But you can't ramble forever."

"True. When the money runs out, I'll have to find a place to settle and start fresh. But I can hold out a year longer, even two if I'm careful. And maybe by then I'll have done enough of the things on my list that I won't feel like I've wasted my life."

"The infamous list," he said with a chuckle.

"It's not *that* infamous," she said, chuckling too.

"Most of my goals are pretty tame. You just happened to see one of the, uh, racier items."

"One? You mean there's something that beats *sex with a stranger?*"

"Of course. Number 14. Or Number 27. Ooh, Number 33 is really hot."

"Okay, okay, I deserved that for teasing you the other day."

"Yes, you did."

"Seriously, Susannah, I can understand your desire to change your life, but did you have to completely give up the old one?"

"There wasn't really anything left to give up."

"What about the friends you left behind?"

"Friends? What friends? By the end of my mother's illness everyone had stopped coming by. They didn't want to sit down in the same room with a woman who poured vinegar on her cornflakes and had a reputation for walking around in nothing but her birthday suit."

"You're serious?"

"Those were good days. She could get away from me and out of the house before I knew what had happened. At night she'd wander off in her nightgown. And she grew increasingly paranoid—she believed I was hurting her or stealing from her. Once I thought she was asleep but she'd somehow managed to crawl out the window. The police found her miles away. When they brought her home she told them I'd tried to kill her.''

''Her own daughter?''

''She didn't know what she was saying or who I was most of the time. Sometimes she'd recognize me. The next hour she'd think I was her nurse. For a while she believed I was her mother.'' His expression made her shake her head. ''Don't feel sorry for me, Ryan. I had a lot of good years with her before she got sick.''

''I'm thankful Nana Sipsey hasn't had those problems. She complains of arthritis in one hip and her hands, but her mind is good. She's still full of spit and fire.''

''Maybe she'll stay that way.''

''Maybe. With luck.'' He finished off his biscuit and dusted the crumbs from his shirt. ''You ready to get to work?''

''Sure. Tell me where you want me to start.''

''Look over what I have on the computer and in the files and begin setting up a workable system for record keeping. Remember, I'm a dummy.''

''I'll make it simple, dummy.''

He playfully tweaked her nose.

''We'll drive down to the center later, and I'll show you where the mural's going. After lunch I'll give you your first lesson.''

''Okay.''

They worked separately for a few hours, he on the design for the mosque, Susannah on the computer. Every now and then she asked a question about a file, but for the most part she left him alone, which he appreciated.

Not that he wasn't aware of her. A man would have to be dead not to be affected by the sexual heat the woman generated.

He knew each time she shifted in her chair or chewed on the end of her pen. The soft sigh she let out when she encountered some crazy thing he'd done raced down his body and settled in his groin.

Other than that, he couldn't complain, at least not about her work. Only once did he have to stop and talk to a customer directly. All the other calls she handled, either taking messages or finding out what the person needed. They had a productive morning.

Close to eleven, Joe ambled in and blew that all to hell. Ryan had asked him to make more shipping crates, and his brother had promised to stop by and get measurements.

Joe grinned widely when he got a good look at Susannah. He ignored Ryan and went straight for her.

"You must be Susannah. I'm Joe."

"Oh, hi!"

"I'm the *handsome* brother."

Susannah giggled and Ryan shook his head. Ten seconds and the kid had charmed her. Amazing.

Had Ryan been so cocky at Joe's age? He didn't think so. Then again, he didn't have Joe's looks or his easygoing way with people.

"Thanks so much for what you did at the cabin yesterday," Susannah told him.

"Glad to help. I've got some firewood for you on the truck. I'll drop it off on my way out. Let me know when you need more."

"Aren't you sweet."

Ryan snorted. Sweet. That was a new one.

"Morning, big brother," Joe called over his shoulder without turning.

"Morning, little brother."

"You didn't tell me Susannah was such a beauty."

"Because I didn't want you over here all the time bothering her."

"Ignore him," Joe said. "Pretend like he's not even here." He took Susannah's hand. "Have dinner with me tonight and we'll go out dancing after."

"And just how old are you?" she asked.

"Twenty-seven."

"Twenty-two," Ryan corrected.

Joe turned and looked at him. "Do you mind? I'm trying to have a conversation with the lady."

"Court on your own time and in your own age

bracket, squirt. I need you to look at those pieces and I don't have all day.''

Joe sighed. "Duty calls. Don't you go away, sweet thing. I'll be right back.''

RYAN'S BROTHER was funny. The two of them together were a riot. Their good-natured bantering as they discussed crates and wrote down measurements amused Susannah. They obviously had a close relationship.

Physically, Joe was a younger, more perfect version of Ryan, at least in the face. He was softer-looking, his features less chiseled. But she couldn't agree he was handsomer. Ryan's maturity added a quality Joe didn't have.

He was shorter and thinner than Ryan, not as well built. He also didn't have his older brother's beautiful hands.

When the two of them were finished, Ryan went back to his worktable, but Joe sat down on the corner of her desk and continued to flirt outrageously.

"Is it true what they say about redheads?'' he asked.

"I don't know. What do they say?''

"That you're all fire and heat.''

Ryan made a noise deep in his throat.

"Did you say something?'' Susannah asked.

"No.''

"So what about dinner?" Joe pressed again.

"Sorry. You're a smidgen too young for me."

"Aw." He clasped his chest with both hands. "Don't reject me."

"I suspect you won't be sitting at home tonight crying."

"Well, probably not," he admitted, grinning. That smile had probably thrown many a female heart into palpitations.

"I'm sure there's some sweet young thing out there who'd love to have you call her up. More than one."

"That's a fact, but I'd rather be with you. I can think of a lot of ways we could entertain each other."

"I'll just bet you can."

Ryan mumbled a remark she couldn't decipher, put down his straight-edge ruler and walked over. "Okay, Romeo, time for you to go." He grabbed him by the collar and lifted him easily to his feet. "Say goodbye."

"Bye, Susannah."

"Bye, Joe."

SUSANNAH LIKED her work, and the day seemed to race by. Around one they picked up sandwiches at Taylor's, the country store. Ryan had a key to the community center, but they didn't need it. A group of women were inside weaving baskets.

Ryan explained they were part of an arts cooperative whose members made native crafts to take to the reservation and sell to tourists during the summer months.

The money raised bought more supplies and helped fund community projects like the ballet class Nia attended, equipment for the volunteer fire station and expansion of the center.

He introduced her, but they didn't linger. He wanted to get back and work a while longer before he had to pick up Nia.

They entered a larger room under construction to the rear. Ryan had brought sketches to show her. She'd already seen three of the five panels back at the workshop, but as he explained where each would go and held up the drawings, she began to understand his vision more clearly.

The mountains were the background and were being done in broken tile of irregular shapes and sizes. Similar tonal values gave them depth and perspective.

A horizontal band about twenty-four inches in height ran midway through each panel. These sections would feature a series of vignettes. Because the subjects included faces and figures, he was putting this part together in what he called *micromosaic* tile. Some of the pieces were smaller than the head of a pin and had to be laid with tweezers.

"Do you see?" he asked. "The people are the heart of the community and will be the heart of the mural. Each person will be represented in a way that others are accustomed to seeing them. Here's the store with Bitsy at the counter and her husband running the cash register. Here are the old men who play dominoes there every afternoon."

As he went through the sketches, he told stories about some of the people. Mrs. McCaffrey, who'd taught school for thirty-five years, would be holding schoolbooks and an apple in the mural. "Doc" Summerfield, a bird watcher, would be shown with his binoculars.

"Ryan, it's wonderful! Do you really know all these people personally?"

"Every one of them."

"How are you handling deaths?"

"All the people living here as of last January when we drew up the construction plans are included, even if they've since died. We've only lost two in that time. We haven't had a birth yet—Helen will be the first this year. Her baby will be our eighty-fifth resident."

"These insets have to be time-consuming to make with pieces of tiles that tiny."

"I've been working on them for ten months in

my spare time. Here's the palette of colors I'm using and this—'' he unfolded a watercolor rendering ''—is basically what it'll look like when it's finished, with a few adjustments. The first panel goes over there and then they progress down that wall, around the corner and across the back.''

The watercolor itself was so beautiful it could have been framed and hanging in a gallery, but the finished mosaic would be stunning.

''I'm overwhelmed,'' she told him. ''This will be incredible.''

''I hope so. One thing I ask. You can't tell anybody what it looks like. A committee approved the general design, but no one will actually see the finished panels until I unveil them at the dedication.''

''I won't give the secret away.''

''When I begin installing, I'll have to keep this inner door locked, but I'm not at that stage yet. The construction crew still has a few things left to finish.''

''What part will I be able to tile?''

''Some of these background areas. They have random pieces you can nip with hand cutters and not have to use the wet saw. I'll show you what I mean when it's time. You need to practice first.''

''I'm excited. I've never been part of anything so beautiful.''

"Hold on to that enthusiasm. You're going to need it over the next few weeks working with me."

THAT AFTERNOON she got her first lesson in grouting, great fun, but harder than she'd imagined. The movement didn't hurt her broken wrist, although she had to hold the little scraper thing just right to get enough of the thick mixture of cement and fine sand to press down between the tiles. She found it easier to push into place with her hands.

Ryan had put together a practice piece so she wouldn't mess anything up.

"Where the hell are your rubber gloves?" he barked, making her jump. He'd been in the back room for the past hour setting up to test-fire some tiles over the weekend and she hadn't heard him approach.

"I can't work with them on. They're too big. The fingers are three inches longer than mine."

"Then you should've said something. You don't want direct contact with grout or any of the adhesives. They all have chemicals in them and they'll eat up your skin."

"Did you explain that?"

"I didn't think I had to. Giving you the gloves and telling you to put them on should've been enough."

"You're right. I'm sorry."

He wiped her fingers with a clean rag until he'd gotten rid of all the excess. Pulling her off her stool to the sink, he doused her hands liberally with vinegar and made her scrub them.

"Being so fair, I'll bet you have sensitive skin, too," he grumbled, handing her a towel. "Some people even have allergic reactions."

She didn't say anything. What *could* she say? She'd done something stupid, and on her very first day of work, too.

The excitement she'd felt only hours earlier dwindled.

Her changed mood must have shown in her face because Ryan's tone softened. He told her not to worry; he'd get her gloves that fit. He had cream that would help if her skin broke out.

"No Powerpuff Girls for you for a week," he teased, smiling tentatively.

Susannah smiled back. "Sorry I screwed up."

"You didn't know any better. Let's clean up and call it a day. I have to go get Nia and you've probably had enough of my foul temper, anyway. Sorry I barked. I'm bad about that."

"That's okay."

"I'm used to working alone. When other people are around, I forget they don't know the fundamentals."

"Or are too stupid to follow directions..."

"Don't sell yourself short. You've been a big help today."

His praise made her feel better.

She cleaned her tools and put the grout in a plastic holding bucket under Ryan's watchful eye. Periodically, he said, once the cement settled to the bottom, he poured away the water and bagged up the residue for disposal. He did the same with the resin-based grouts and adhesives so as not to mess up the plumbing.

She tidied the workbench.

"I meant to ask if I could take some photographs while we're working. I've been documenting my travels and posting photos on my Web site. I'd love to include shots of you, along with some of the finished pieces."

"I don't know about me, but I have no problem with your shooting the mosaics. Are you any good? I wouldn't mind having copies."

"Very good. Actually it's the camera that's good, a very high resolution five megapixel that gives quality comparable to a 35 mm SLR."

"I have no idea what you just said."

"Any dummy can take a clear, brilliant photo with it."

"Now you're speaking my language."

"The images are digital, meaning we can plug the camera into your computer or mine and import them for dropping into Web pages, brochures to send out, business cards. Everything's instantaneous. No film to develop.''

''I know nothing about this stuff.''

''The technology today is amazing. Have you considered setting up a Web site to advertise?''

''Joe's tried to get me to do it. He has one for the furniture he makes. But I already have too many contracts and my business is nearly all word of mouth, anyway. I'm not sure a Web site would help me much.''

''You may be right. To hire someone to set up and maintain it can get expensive. But you wouldn't need anything complicated—only simple informational pages to highlight your work and let potential customers know how to contact you. Those aren't difficult to design yourself if you have the right program. It's all wizzie wig.''

''Remember who you're talking to.''

''W-Y-S-I-W-Y-G. What You See Is What You Get. The program has a graphical interface. You design the page the way you want it to look, and the program automatically generates the HTML code, or language, needed to display it to visitors.''

''If you say so.''

''You're technologically challenged now, but by the time I get through with you, you're going to be a different man.''

"Don't count on it. I can't even figure out how to set the answering machine to catch my calls."

"I know, but I fixed that already. I recorded a message and set it to pick up after six rings."

"Are you always so efficient?"

"Yes, or so I'm told. I have one of those structured minds that thrives on order. Being able to file and categorize today—I've been in heaven."

"I'm the opposite. Anything orderly frightens me."

"We should make a good team, then. You create the chaos and I'll have fun cleaning it up."

They both laughed.

He followed her out and locked the door.

"Friday is usually pizza night for me and Nia," he said. "Come with us."

"I'd like to, but I need to buy groceries and wash clothes. I thought I'd go to town now before it gets dark."

"We can stop and pick up your groceries while we're out. And you can use the washer and dryer upstairs any time. No use paying a laundry. Throw them in when we get back."

"Okay, but only if you promise to let me buy the pizza, since you cooked last night."

"I'll flip you for it at the restaurant."

"IF YOU WIN, you shouldn't have to pay," Susannah argued, picking up the bill from the table.

"*Because* I won, I get the right to choose." Ryan reached across and snatched the slip of paper from her hand. "I choose to pay."

"I've never played the game like that."

"Then you haven't been doing it right."

Next to Susannah in the booth, Nia giggled.

"What's so funny?" Susannah asked. She tickled the child's side. "You sure do have a bad case of the sillies tonight."

"You and Daddy are funny. You fuss all the time."

"He's the funny one. Look how his head is all lopsided. And his nose sticks out so far we might have to put a flag on the end so cars won't run into it."

Nia giggled again. "Nah-ah. My daddy is beautiful."

"Beautiful? You think so?"

"Uh-huh."

"Well, let's see." She studied Ryan's face. His eyebrows lifted in question, waiting for her response. "You know, I think you're right. He *is* beautiful in a weird, lopsided, long-nosed kind of way."

"Thanks a lot," he said.

Nia yanked on her sleeve.

"I know a secret about Daddy's quarter."

"What kind of secret?"

Nia looked at him. He shook his head.

"I can't tell."

"Oh, I get it. He tricked me somehow, didn't he?"

"Uh-huh, it's got a man on both—" Nia slapped her hands over her mouth, realizing she'd almost given away what she knew.

Susannah pretended to be mad at him. She held out her palm. "Okay, buster, show me the quarter."

"Not on your life."

"You don't play fair."

"As fair as you."

"You flipped the coin *and* you called first."

"So?"

"So that's not how you do it."

"Next time we'll use *your* quarter and *I'll* call first."

"Okay," she said, then realized he'd tricked her again and sputtered, "Wait a minute, that's not right."

"You already agreed. Too late."

They argued again at the grocery store when Ryan tried to pay for a pair of rubber gloves she bought for work. The man had a streak of hardheadedness in him. This time, he gave in because she threatened to slug him.

Her hands were a little dry and itchy from the

exposure to the grout. She didn't tell Ryan, only added a bottle of moisturizing cream to her basket.

They checked out, and he loaded her groceries into the truck's back seat with Nia. ''Do you need anything else while we're in town?'' he asked, getting in.

''I got everything.''

''Anyplace you want to stop?''

''Can't think of one.''

Robbinsville was a sweet place, nestled in a valley among the mountains, but Susannah couldn't see much to do after dark. During the quick tour Ryan gave her, she admired the courthouse made of native stone. Ryan showed her the sheriff's office where Bass worked.

The surrounding ''downtown'' of a handful of streets was quaint and had some interesting antique and period clothing shops, but all were closed now. Tomorrow she'd drive back and have a better look around in daylight, maybe see if she could find another pair of jeans.

The only road with any traffic was a one-street ''bypass'' with a few fast-food restaurants, a couple of motels and a convenience store. Ryan stopped at the store and pulled up to the pumps to get gas.

While he was inside paying, Nia took off her seat belt and leaned over to talk to Susannah.

''When are we going to make the brownies?'' she

asked. Susannah had bought a boxed mix at the store.

"Maybe this weekend, but first we have to see if your grandmother will let us borrow a pan. Your daddy isn't sure he has one that'll work."

"My friend Mary is making banana splits at her sleep-over party tomorrow."

"Then we should wait to make brownies another time. Eating brownies and banana splits on the same day wouldn't be good."

"Daddy says I don't have to go to the party if I don't want to."

"But you want to go, don't you?" Nia didn't seem too sure. "You're not too young to start spending the night away from home. And sleep-overs are great fun. I went to a lot of them when I was a little girl."

"But what happens if you miss your daddy?"

"You'll be playing so many games and laughing so much, you won't have time to miss him. But if you *were* to miss him, you could always call."

"I could come home?"

"If you really, really felt you had to, I guess he could drive over and get you, but I don't think you'd want to leave."

"What if I got sick?"

"Of course you could come home if you got sick,

but you're feeling okay now, aren't you?'' She said she was. "Then I wouldn't worry."

"Susannah?'' Nia's demeanor turned more serious. She obviously had something else to ask, but seemed reluctant to continue.

"What is it, sweetheart?"

"If Daddy doesn't want me anymore and gives me away, can I come live with you?"

"Doesn't want...?'' The question stunned her. If ever a child was doted on and loved, it was this one. Her father adored her. That was obvious to anyone who saw them together.

"Nia, that's not something you ever have to worry about. Your daddy loves you very much. He'd never give you away."

"But if he did, would you let me be your little girl?"

Susannah had no idea how to answer.

SHE DEBATED whether she should tell Ryan about her conversation with his daughter. Nia had seemed genuinely worried about her father giving her away. Yet all young children had fears about being unwanted, didn't they?

She could remember feeling that way herself a few times as a child. Once she'd gotten in trouble for coloring on the wall of the freshly painted living room. Convinced her mother wouldn't want her anymore, she'd run away—as far as the neighbor's back porch.

The child had no reason to worry. Ryan loved her. Still…something didn't seem quite right in the Whitepath household.

Nia didn't go to her party Saturday night and she also backed out of baking brownies. She didn't feel good, she said, but her complaints were vague. First it was her head, then her stomach, then both her head and her stomach.

Ryan said not to be concerned. She did this sometimes.

"I think she was afraid she'd get homesick at the sleep-over and embarrass herself in front of her friends," he said.

Susannah decided that was reasonable, but it didn't explain why Nia didn't want to be around *her*.

She felt she'd handled her answer to the child's question poorly. As much as she'd love Nia to be her little girl, she'd told the child, she wasn't planning on ever being a mommy.

Nia was herself again on Sunday morning when Susannah joined the family for church. Later, during dinner at Ryan's mother's house, Joe and Nia told jokes to each other and laughed throughout the meal, making Nana Sipsey threaten to take a switch to both of them. Nia seemed completely recovered.

"Annie, this roast is delicious," Susannah told her.

Everyone echoed the sentiment.

"Thank you. How did you enjoy the service? Was it very different from what you're used to?"

"A little different, but interesting." A few of the hymns were the same, sung in Cherokee or English. The program had provided a translation of the Cherokee prayers.

The best part, though, was seeing Ryan dressed in a suit.

"Daddy has Susannah's underpants in his pocket," Nia suddenly announced.

Ryan nearly choked on his food.

Every person at the table stopped eating and stared at him.

"Do tell," Joe said with a grin.

"Uh, I found them in the dryer," Ryan explained when he'd stopped coughing. His face had turned crimson. Susannah imagined her face was the same lovely shade. "She washed her clothes over at our place the other night."

"That's a good one, brother," Joe told him.

"Joseph!" His mother warned him to behave.

Susannah was mortified, especially when Ryan later took the silky scrap of red fabric from the pocket of his jacket and handed it to her.

"Nice color," was all he said.

CHAPTER EIGHT

SUSANNAH FELL into a routine at work and the first month passed swiftly. Before she knew it, her time in Sitting Dog was already half gone.

Thanksgiving came. The Whitepaths didn't observe the holiday, but Ryan's brother Charlie, his wife and their two boys drove over from Winston-Salem to visit for the day. His sister came home from college for the weekend.

Ryan's mother invited the man she'd been dating, Bob Humphreys, over for everyone to meet.

Susannah tried to keep to her cabin and not intrude on the family's time together, but they insisted on including her.

As it turned out, there *was* cause for celebration. Helen Miller went into labor and gave birth to a healthy little girl.

Margaret Ann Miller, weighing eight pounds and one ounce, burst into the world Saturday afternoon. That night, Ryan and Susannah drove to the hospital in Andrews to see mother and baby.

Susannah couldn't say she was close to Helen.

Twice she'd brought her meals at Annie's request. Three or four times, when Ryan had driven over to talk to Bass or check on Helen while Bass was at work, Susannah had ridden along with him.

Once, she'd picked up Nia from the bus stop and the two of them had dropped by with a basket for Helen. It was hand-woven by Nana and contained two loaves of banana-nut bread.

She liked the woman. With more time to develop a friendship, she sensed the two of them might become close.

When she and Ryan arrived, Helen was sitting up in the bed holding baby Maggie in her arms.

"She's the spitting image of her daddy," Bass crowed proudly over his newborn daughter.

"She's too pretty to look like you," Ryan told him. He kissed Helen on the forehead. "I'm proud of you. How are you feeling? Okay?"

"A little sore, but much better than this morning. Any woman who says childbirth is a good kind of pain is a liar."

Susannah laid presents on the bed. "This is from Annie and Nana Sipsey. I think you'll love what they did. They've been working on something for the baby. The rectangular package is from Ryan."

"And Susannah," he added quickly. "She helped me pick it out."

"Nia made you a card," Susannah said. "And

Anita told me to tell you she'd come by tomorrow before she heads back to school. She also has a little something for you."

"That's so nice. Open the gifts for me, would you, please?"

Ryan's mother and Nana had crocheted a darling white outfit and matching blanket. Susannah had suggested Ryan get something for Helen rather than the baby, since giving birth could be tiring and emotional. They'd shopped on the way over and found an exquisite bed-jacket in a colorful Asian print.

"How gorgeous! Ryan, you doll! And thank you, Susannah, for helping him choose this. I love it!"

"You're welcome."

"Ryan, please thank your mother and grandmother for me. And tell Nia her card was exactly what I needed."

"I will."

Helen wanted to try nursing the baby again, so Ryan and Bass went outside, where Bass planned to smoke one of the pink-wrapped cigars he'd been handing out. Susannah stayed with Helen.

"Neither one of us has gotten the hang of this yet," Helen explained. "The nurses said not to worry, though." After several attempts, the baby finally latched on and began to suckle. Helen brushed her hand softly, lovingly across the tiny dark head. "That's my good girl."

"She really is beautiful," Susannah said. "She has your features, I think, but her skin is the same lovely brown as Bass's."

"Some people wouldn't call it lovely."

"Your parents?"

"Susannah, they haven't even bothered to find out if Maggie and I are okay. Can you believe that? What kind of people could ignore their own grandchild?"

"Maybe they're on the way down from Pennsylvania."

"I wish that was true, but it's not. Even though he didn't want to, I forced Bass to call them when we got to the hospital. They said they didn't care to know about the *half-breed* child and hung up on him."

"Oh, Helen, I'm so sorry."

"If it was only me I wouldn't care." Her eyes filled with tears. "But I don't want my daughter to grow up thinking there's something wrong with her because of her Native American blood. And I hate that they've treated Bass so horribly. They've hardly been civil to him in the five years we've been married. I've kept in touch. I prayed that one day... But when I told them I was pregnant, they even stopped talking to me on the phone."

She broke down and cried. Susannah sat next to

her on the bed, put an arm around her shoulders and tried to comfort her.

"I can't begin to understand why they feel the way they do, but Helen, you have to accept that it's *their* problem. You have a great husband who's crazy about you and a beautiful new baby. If your mom and dad don't want to know them, I'm not sure what you can do to change that. Feel sorry for them. Keep hoping they'll change. But don't let them ruin your happiness."

"You're absolutely right." She wiped her eyes. "I shouldn't let it get to me. I'm probably feeling a bit of postpartum depression. Hold the baby for me a minute, will you? I need to wash my face before Bass comes back. I don't want him to know I've been crying."

Susannah looked at the tiny bundle with horror. "Don't you want to put her in the bassinet?"

"Are you afraid of her?"

"Honestly? Yes. I'm terrified. I've never held a baby before."

"Never?"

"I was an only child. I never even did any baby-sitting. I know zero about kids."

"But you're so wonderful with Nia. That day the two of you dropped by, she was as lively and happy as I've seen her in ages."

"Nia's an exception. I feel comfortable around

her because…I don't know. I was going to say because she's old enough to reason with, but that's not always the case.''

"Maybe you're comfortable because you've grown to care about her?''

"I suppose that's true. She can be moody and she gets her feelings hurt easily, but most of the time she's great fun to be around. I enjoy her. Babies— now that's a new experience for me.''

"For me, too, but Bass and I plan on having a houseful. And we're also going to adopt. We're waiting for a child right now.''

"Are you? That's wonderful!''

"So many children out there need homes.''

Helen tried to hand the baby to her again.

Susannah shook her head. "Helen, I'm not sure about this. I might drop her.''

"You won't. Besides, you *have* to take her. I'm too sore to get out of this bed and hold her at the same time.''

Helen passed over the warm bundle and Susannah accepted her with trepidation.

"See, it's not so scary,'' Helen said. She struggled to sit and swing her legs over the side of the bed. She eased to a standing position and put on her robe and slippers.

"Do you need help? I can buzz for the nurse.''

"No, I can do it. The doctor said I should get up

and begin taking short walks. This will do me good.''

Susannah sat in the chair and cradled Maggie to her chest while Helen took short, shuffling steps to the bathroom. Having the small body in her arms felt good, felt right somehow. Susannah had to admit the sensation wasn't at all unpleasant.

''You're an angel,'' she told her. The baby's face was red and wrinkly and she had scratches on her cheeks where her fingernails had raked them, but she was adorable. She had a full head of dark hair, which Susannah found amazing.

''How is everything with Ryan?'' Helen called out. ''Are you enjoying working with him?''

''Very much. He's a great teacher. I only wish I had a tenth of his talent.''

Helen came back a few minutes later with her hair combed and her face washed. She'd taken the time to put on a little lipstick.

''Ryan's a good person,'' she said, sitting slowly down on the bed. ''Not too many single men would've taken on the responsibility of raising a child. And he's doing a wonderful job with Nia.''

Susannah agreed. ''He's a good father.''

''I remember the first time I met him. Bass and I weren't married yet, but we'd gotten serious. I already had a pretty good idea I wanted to marry him. I was living out of town and I came down for the weekend to suffer through the big introduction to his parents and friends. Boy, was I nervous. But Ryan was wonderful. He treated me like he'd known me all his life.''

"He has a way of doing that.''

"Nia was about two months old then, I guess. Here was this big muscular guy with this tiny baby strapped to his chest. They were so cute.''

"I'd love to have seen that.''

"I have pictures at the house. Remind me next time you're over and I'll show them to you.''

"Oh, I'm glad you said that. I nearly forgot. I brought my camera.''

She handed Maggie back to Helen.

"Do you mind getting a few of Bass and the baby before you leave?'' Helen asked after Susannah had taken multiple shots. "He recorded the birth with the video camera, but I'd love some stills.''

"Of course not. And we can do a family photo with the three of you, if you want.''

"I'd love a family photo! I could put copies in my birth announcements. Let me know how much I owe you for the prints.''

"Don't worry about it. Once you get home and settled, I'll bring over my computer and we'll look at all the shots. You can decide which ones you like. The prints will be my gift.''

"You're incredibly nice. I understand why Ryan's so crazy about you."

Her comment piqued Susannah's interest. "What makes you think that?"

"The way he looks at you. The expression on his face when he talks about you."

"When has he talked about me?"

"One night when he dropped over to the house. He said you're a hard worker."

Susannah sighed inwardly. How disappointing. Not the most flattering of remarks.

"He also said he likes having you around. You make him laugh."

Ugh! That was little improvement over *hard worker*.

"He makes me laugh, too," Susannah told her.

"I sense he's conflicted about his feelings. You won't be here that much longer, and that's a problem. But if you gave him the slightest indication you were interested in him, he'd probably overlook his worries and make a move."

"You're mistaken, Helen. Ryan and I are only friends. He's never even hinted that he's attracted to me."

"Hasn't he?"

"A couple of times I thought... No, I'm sure it was only my imagination."

"Maybe I'm asking the wrong question here. Are *you* attracted to *him?*"

Susannah opened her mouth to deny it, but she couldn't. With each passing day she'd grown to respect Ryan more and more, not only for his talent, but for the honorable way in which he conducted his business and for the loving way he treated his family.

From a physical standpoint, she found it hard to look at him without imagining a few naughty things she'd like to do.

He had this old pair of overalls he wore when he was firing tiles. She'd never thought of overalls as sexy until she'd seen them on Ryan Whitepath, both clasps undone so the bib hung down. With his shirt off, skin glistening with sweat, chest and arm muscles bulging, she found it hard to watch him and breathe at the same time.

Her silence made Helen chuckle.

"I thought so. You *are* attracted to him. Now, my next question is, what do you plan to do about it?"

"CUTE BABY, isn't she?" Ryan said when the silence in the truck became too much. Susannah had hardly spoken a word since they left the hospital.

"Very cute."

"Anything wrong? You're pretty quiet tonight."

"Nothing's wrong."

"Tired?"

"Not particularly."

There was obviously something on her mind, but he let it drop. He took her to the door of the cabin and said good-night, then hurried to the house to collect Nia.

His grandmother was reading a magazine while watching TV. At eighty-two she could still follow both the article and the show.

"Elisi." He leaned down and kissed her.

She patted his arm. *"Gvgeyu."* I love you.

His sister, she said, had gone out to see friends.

Ryan found his mother in the kitchen, trying to deal with leftover food. Nia had already been put to bed. She urged him not to disturb her.

"Let her sleep. If you wake her now, you might have trouble getting her back down."

"I'll sleep here, then. If she has a nightmare..."

"When was her last one?"

"A couple of weeks ago."

"She's better. You said the doctor told you as much."

"Dr. Thompson said she *seemed* better. Nia was more talkative the last visit. And she didn't cry like she normally does."

"Ogedoda has heard your prayers. Your daughter is healing."

"I want to believe that, but I'm afraid to get my hopes up."

"Have hope, but remember that difficult problems take time to correct themselves. Be patient."

"I'll try."

"It's early. Go out and have fun for a change. Sleep at your own house so you can rest. Let me watch my granddaughter."

"I shouldn't." He rubbed the back of his neck, feeling the tension there.

"You've been working too hard. A young man needs the company of other young people. For once, follow Joseph's example."

"I don't believe you're telling me to act like *Joe.*"

"Your brother is young and often foolish, but at least *he* knows how to relax. Isn't there a young woman who would enjoy your company for the night?"

"*Etsi!*"

She chuckled at his shocked face. "You think I'm so old I don't understand the comfort of lying in someone's arms?"

"Yes! I mean, no!"

Hell! Did she have to go and put an image of *that* in his head? Every time he looked at Bob Humphreys from now on, he'd think of his mother having sex with the guy.

"I get your point without the illustrations," he told her.

He felt guilty about leaving. He worried that Nia might wake up and need him. But he could use a break. And it was still early, not yet nine o'clock.

"Okay, I'll go out for a little while, but I'll keep my cell phone on. Call if anything happens."

"I will. Now, off with you. And if I should wake up early in the morning and see your truck parked down at the cabin, I will pretend not to notice."

Ryan swore under his breath. The sly old bird. She'd set him up.

HE HEADED DOWN the drive, telling himself he wouldn't give in to his desires and go to Susannah's. He'd see if Bass had gotten home yet. They'd shoot pool and smoke a few cigars.

Not until he'd parked at the cabin did he admit to himself that this was his intended destination all along. So many nights he'd wanted to come here, but he'd stopped himself.

He didn't get out immediately. After he turned off the engine, he sat there for several minutes. In a month, she'd be gone. He had no business being here, starting something that had no future.

He got out and walked up to the porch.

No damn business at all.

He lifted his hand to knock, but before he could, the door swung open.

"I wondered if you were going to stay out there all night," she said.

"I was…thinking."

"About whether or not you should come in?"

He nodded slowly. "I'm not sure being alone with you like this is a good idea."

"Yet here you are."

"Yeah, here I am."

She stepped aside and he entered. Somehow she'd made the cabin seem like her own. Little touches of her were everywhere—oranges and apples in a bowl on the table, a branch of evergreen draped across the mantel.

She'd created cardboard frames to display photographs she'd taken of the family and hung a patchwork quilt on the wall.

The couch and table had been pushed back, and she'd placed a small rug he didn't recognize in front of the hearth.

"I was about to try starting a fire," she said.

"Let me do it."

He brought in logs. In the wood box he scavenged until he found a thin piece of lighter, a resin-filled shard of pine he used to ignite the kindling. Within a few minutes, he had a blaze going.

Taking her lead, he sat down on the rug, his arm propped across his knee.

"Are you in a no-furniture mode?" he asked.

"I like it better on the floor. That's why I scooted the couch back from the fireplace." She smiled. "Sometimes I get silly and pretend it's 1850. I light the oil lamp and read a book by its light. I imagine there's no electricity or computers or microwaves."

"Strange behavior for a techno-geek like you."

"I suppose it is, but since I've been here, I've come to appreciate a simpler way of life."

"Tomorrow I'll help you toss out your computer."

"I don't think I'm ready for *that* drastic a step."

"I'd say it's a good thing you didn't really live here in the 1850s. You would never have survived it."

"Oh, I don't know. Raising my own food, cooking over an open fire… Sounds like fun, don't you think?"

"What about giving birth without a doctor in case you had problems? Having to climb the mountain on foot to visit a neighbor? Or kill a deer and skin it so your kids won't starve?"

"Uh, okay. Not so much fun. But I still admire the relationship people used to have with the environment. They depended on it for their survival. Folks today don't appreciate the natural world as much. I'm ashamed to admit I was one of them until I came to visit this mountain."

"When I was younger, my grandfather used to take me into the backcountry and tell me stories about the First People and how, through the grace of *Elohi,* the mother spirit of the earth, they lived in peace with her. Everything they needed was provided—food, skins, medicines. In return, the people protected her, honored her."

"That's the way it should be."

"I've watched my grandmother in her garden, gathering her leaves and roots, and each time she takes something from the earth she thanks it. Each spring she makes me plant trees and scatter seeds in the nearby woods to make up for what *Elohi* gives our family."

"We should all live like your grandmother. She's a very intuitive woman."

"Yes, she is."

"She spooked me a bit when I first got here, the way she seemed to know how people were feeling without being told. I figured out it's because she's such a good listener. And she notices things that others don't."

"Listen or your tongue will make you deaf. It's an old Cherokee saying."

"I like that."

"Nana's ancestors were all Medicine Elders of

the *Ani Wodi* clan, as is she. She was raised to understand natural, physical and spiritual healing.''

"I love sitting at the kitchen table with her while we're preparing supper and talking.''

"She likes that, too. She's told me so.''

"And her stories are wonderful. I don't understand half the words, but somehow I know what she's trying to tell me. The other day she was talking about turtles.''

"Ah, how turtle got the lines on his shell.''

"That's it. Another day, it was why the possum's tail is bare.''

"And why he plays dead?''

"Yes. I'll miss my visits with Nana when I leave. I'll miss her.''

"Is she the only one you'll miss?''

She looked away. "You know she isn't. I've grown to care about all of you.''

He traced the line of her jaw with his index finger, turning her head to make her look at him again. "Any of us more than others?''

"Yes.''

He slipped his hand behind her head and pulled her forward for a gentle kiss. Sweet. He knew it would be. The second time he pressed harder, demanded more, and like the flower that opens wider with the warmth of sun, so did her lips. She welcomed him inside.

Desire raced through him. She was forbidden, dangerous, and every cell in his brain warned him he should back away. But he couldn't force himself. He wanted her. Almost from that first day, when he'd watched as she read with his daughter, he'd ached to feel her body against his.

Four long weeks he'd endured the torture of hearing her laugh, witnessing the way her face lit up when she was having fun or learning something new.

He'd come to care about her a little more with each passing day, but aside from that, he'd come to *enjoy* her. She was funny. She amused him. He looked forward to getting up each morning because he knew he'd be with Susannah.

"Mmm," she murmured as the kiss ended. She opened her eyes and smiled softly. "That was as nice as I imagined it would be."

"Have you been thinking about my kissing you?"

"At least a hundred times a day."

"You should've said something. I might have done it sooner."

"No, you wouldn't have. You're as afraid of me as I am of you. Maybe even more so. You have Nia's feelings to worry about. I only have my own."

"Starting a relationship with no future is pretty crazy."

"I agree."

"I don't want to hurt you. I don't want to *get* hurt."

"I feel the same way," she told him. "But if we both understand it isn't permanent, how can anyone get hurt?"

He gazed into her eyes and saw a reflection of his own heart. This woman was his life mate. He knew it suddenly with a clarity that astounded him.

"What's wrong?" she asked. "You have the strangest look on your face."

"Nothing." He shook his head.

If this was meant to be, then he had to trust that somehow it would work out. And he couldn't be with her without honesty.

"Susannah?"

"Yes, Ryan?"

"I have things to tell you and you're probably not going to like hearing them. But if we're going to have any kind of relationship, I don't want any lies or secrets between us."

"That sounds ominous. What is it?"

"Since Nia's mother died, she hasn't been herself. She worries when she's separated from me. Emotionally she's...ill. When I sometimes disappear on Monday afternoons, I take her to a doctor for treatment of depression and anxiety. In addition to the nightmares, she has panic attacks. Bad ones."

"I had no idea her problems were so serious."

"Yeah, well, I've hidden it from you as much as I could. I'm not proud to tell anyone I've failed my daughter."

"You have no reason to be ashamed. It isn't your fault."

"I feel like it is. I should be able to make her feel better, to prove to her that everything's going to be all right."

"Ryan, that's not always the way it works. Illnesses like Nia's are caused by chemical imbalances in the brain, and they can be brought on by a trauma. I struggled with depression and anxiety myself when my mother died. I felt terrible guilt for being glad that I no longer had to take care of her. For weeks I could barely leave the house."

"How did you get past it?"

"With medication and therapy. Is Nia taking anything?"

"Not at the moment. We're holding out until after the first of the year to see if her condition improves. The doctor said a lot of the adult drugs haven't been tested for pediatric use, or have bad side effects."

"What about a support group? She might benefit from interacting with other children who've also lost parents."

"We tried that with a group in Charlottesville. Nia didn't want to go. Forcing her only made the panic attacks worse."

"Poor little thing."

"There's more. And it has to do with you. Will you promise to keep an open mind and not get mad? You seemed my best hope."

"Your best...?" She stopped suddenly. "Oh, wait. You expected *me* to help her?"

"She responds to you. She likes you."

"And I like her. But Ryan, I'm not a therapist! I'm not trained to handle the problems of a sick child. And I told you when you hired me that I'd be leaving soon."

Obviously agitated, she jumped up. Ryan also got to his feet.

"I didn't—don't—expect you to handle her problems. Dr. Thompson thought it would be good for her just to be around someone who's dealing with the same kind of loss."

"Oh, great. You talked to Nia's doctor about me?"

"Nia did—she mentioned her new friend. But yes, the doctor and I have had a few conversations in which you were the subject. She felt you'd be a positive influence on Nia. And you have been."

"This is why you so abruptly changed your mind and decided to hire me, isn't it? You and the good doctor had a little chat and decided to conspire against me."

"Dr. Thompson assumes I discussed this with

you, so I'm the one at fault, not her. I'm sorry for not leveling with you. I wanted to, but I was afraid if I did you'd leave."

"I would have. I can't believe you've done this. It's not fair, Ryan."

"Come on, Susannah. Have I asked you to do anything special for Nia in the past few weeks? You've picked her up at the bus stop, but other than that, have I asked you to do anything you normally wouldn't?"

"No, not really."

"You're a good person with a good heart. You've played with her, read her stories and been her friend because you *wanted* to, not because I asked you to."

"All right, I admit that's true, but you shouldn't have schemed against me. I don't like being used."

"I'm sorry. You deserve better. And once you came to work, I realized how much I needed you, too. What can I do to make this up to you?"

"I'll have to think about it."

"Do you want me to leave?"

"Maybe." Her expression softened. "No," she said, shaking her head.

He let out his breath. "So am I forgiven?"

"I don't know yet. Ask me again in a little while."

CHAPTER NINE

THEY TALKED for a long time. Susannah found it hard to stay angry with Ryan when she knew he was only trying to help his daughter.

He told her frightening stories, about Nia's panic attacks and about the dreams that terrified her but that she could never remember.

"Never?"

"No, she wakes up screaming for me. I don't know if she's being chased or hurt in those dreams. And she's gotten it into her head that I might abandon her, which sends her into a panic when I'm out of her sight for more than a few hours. Keeping her in school has been hell, although she's been better about that since you got here. She's been better about a lot of things...."

"She asked me once if she could be my little girl if you gave her away."

"When was this?"

"Soon after I came here. That first time we went grocery shopping. You were paying for your gas. She leaned over the seat and dropped that bombshell on me. I was concerned about it, but then shrugged it off as normal childhood anxiety. Now I realize I should have told you. I'm sorry.''

''It doesn't matter. I already know she's frightened. The question is *why?* The doctor says it was triggered by Carla's death.''

''I wish I knew what to do.''

''Being able to talk to you has helped a lot. I try not to tell Mom and Nana too much. They worry.''

''You can talk to me anytime.''

He threaded his fingers through hers. ''That jerk you were engaged to…what was his name?''

''Andrew.''

''Andrew was a fool to give you up.''

He kissed her and warmth eased into every part of her body. As insane as it was, she wound her arms around his neck and drew him closer.

''It feels like maybe you've forgiven me,'' he said against her lips.

''You think so?''

He urged her down to the floor.

''If you don't want me to make love to you, tell me to go home now.''

She gave him his answer by undoing his buttons, then sliding her hands across his naked chest.

"Last chance. If you don't want me to make love to you…"

She smiled and began removing his pants.

RYAN TREMBLED with the touch of her fingers on his zipper. He tried his best to be patient, but he'd never wanted a woman more than this one and she was undressing him so damn slow.

"Here, let me help you," he offered, quickly discarding his boots, socks and jeans.

"A bit anxious, aren't we?" she teased. "Can *I* do the rest?"

"Go ahead."

She slowly lowered his briefs. As he kissed her, he helped her undo the buttons on her shirt and shed her jeans. She dragged her nails lightly along his ribs, across his stomach and down his thighs, skimming his growing erection with each pass, but not lingering on it. He decided she was intentionally trying to drive him crazy—and succeeding.

Her panties were hot pink and matched her bra. She lay on her side facing him, the firelight making her pale skin seem translucent.

"I like your freckles," he said. "Are they everywhere?"

"I don't know. I've never really thought about it."

"I'll look and see."

He removed the rest of her clothes. She giggled as he rolled her onto her stomach and conducted a thorough inspection of every inch of her back and legs.

"Well?" she asked. "What's the verdict?"

"Yep, they're all over everything on this side. They even make pictures. You have a flower right down here." He kissed the small of her back. "And right here—" he touched his lips to the back of one of her knees "—you have a cloud."

"That feels so good. Where else?"

He pretended to find bears and trees and dogs. He kissed every one.

She turned over, and her eyes had become heavy-lidded with desire. "And what about this side? Any interesting pictures on it?"

"A thousand."

"Will you kiss them, too?"

"Gladly."

"I know there are a couple right here," she said, touching her breasts. He kissed both rosy tips. "And here," she said, indicating the insides of her thighs. Her back arched from the floor when he kissed her there. "Oh, Ryan! I'd forgotten how wonderful it feels to make love."

"How long has it been for you?"

"Two years."

It had been about that long for him, too. Since Nia came to live with him, he hadn't dated much or given sex priority. He enjoyed it, and sometimes physically his body needed it, but in the seven-year stretch between Carla and Susannah, he hadn't felt attracted to anyone, and sex had been more of a chore than a pleasure.

He wasn't going to last long this first time and neither was she, so they brought each other quickly to climax. With that out of the way, they were free to take their time, to enjoy the slow road back to arousal.

At least, he *thought* the journey was going to be slow. He was wrong. When she gave him a massage, he tried to give her one, but she squirmed under his palms and decided she'd had enough foreplay.

"Make love to me," she said, guiding him.

"Yes, ma'am. Whatever you want."

The floor wasn't the most comfortable place to do this, but after a couple of minutes he no longer cared. Susannah delighted him by being a very vocal lover. She wasn't shy about asking for what she wanted or letting him know she was enjoying herself. Pretty soon he was spiraling out of control, no longer able to hold back.

But he didn't need to. She came with him. Her climax exploded within seconds of his. The pleasure was so pure and so intense, he was afraid it had stopped his heart.

"Mmm, that was incredible," she said. "I wouldn't mind doing that a hundred more times tonight."

Ryan groaned. "Give me a few minutes to rest and then I'll see what I can do."

SUSANNAH TRIED to move but Ryan had his leg partly over hers. He'd pinned her to the mattress. Thank God they'd moved to the bed the second time they'd made love. That hard floor had nearly broken her bones.

He mumbled in his sleep and grasped her left breast. In the pale light from the dying fire, his brown hand looked strange against her white flesh.

He was all hard sculptured muscle, a living work of art, and she'd never seen anything more beautiful in her life.

His body fascinated her, from the long hair that draped her like a tent when he made love, to his cute bony toes.

He was perfectly made and flawless, except for one scar. Stitches, he'd told her. He'd fallen from a tree and cut open his right knee when he was seven.

With Andrew, sex had been enjoyable, but it had always included questions afterward: "Was that good? Did you come?"

Sometimes she'd wanted to scream at him, "Stop with the quiz! This isn't school!"

Ryan didn't have to ask. He'd known by her cry that she'd enjoyed every spiraling wave of ecstasy.

He stirred, opened his eyes and saw she was awake. "Sorry, I must've dozed off. What time is it?"

"Midnight."

"I should go home."

"Probably." She stroked his shoulder. "I don't want your mother knowing what we've been doing for the last two hours."

He chuckled and rolled onto his back.

"What's so funny?"

"I doubt she'd be surprised."

"That may be true, but we shouldn't change how we act in front of your family, and our working relationship needs to stay professional."

"Can I carry your panties around in my pocket while I work?"

"No!"

"Dadgum. That's the only reason I slept with you. I was hoping you'd give me a pair."

She sat up so she could talk to him. "You're such a comedian. I don't know how I stand you."

"You stood me just fine a while ago—twice."

"I was only humoring you. I don't really find you all that attractive."

"Oh, is that right?" He pulled her down on top of him. "So how come you begged me to make love to you?"

"*Begged* you? You're having a hallucination, mister."

"Oh, Ryan, touch me there," he said in a high feminine voice, imitating exactly how she'd sounded during lovemaking. "That feels so good. And you're so huge."

She laughed so hard she had to put her head down on his chest. "You added the 'huge.' I didn't say that."

"Okay, I embellished a bit."

The body part under discussion was currently rigid against her leg and demanding attention. One slight movement, and she'd be in trouble.

As much as she wanted to make love to him again, they had a major problem. They'd used both of the small packets in his wallet.

"Uh, before you get too worked up, remember we have no more condoms."

"Ah, hell."

"Sorry, but I don't have any. And I don't think we should take the risk of not using one. This is a safe time for me, but accidents can happen."

"Yeah, I was conceived in this bed."

"Oh, boy, I forgot about that. Then we'd better not tempt the spirits."

"You're right."

She expected him to get up. Instead, he rolled and took her with him, reversing their positions. Now she was on the bottom.

He sought out the soft red curls between her legs

and stroked beneath them with his fingers. Slick with her own moisture and on fire, she feared she might spontaneously combust, but he wouldn't let her come. Again and again, he'd let her get close, but not go over the edge.

"Are you trying to kill me?" she croaked out.

"Yes."

The next time, he waited until she was a breath away and replaced his fingers with his mouth. Tremors shook her whole body. Even after she climaxed, he continued to make love to her with his lips and tongue.

A second and a third wave of incredible pleasure washed along her nerve endings.

"Oh!"

She really *had* died.

And gone to heaven.

When she could speak and move again, she told him she'd do the same for him, but he said no.

"That was a gift. Gifts should always be given because you want to, not because you expect the other person to reciprocate."

"I feel a bit stingy getting and not giving."

"Nothing says sex has to be equal."

She nodded. "I'll give you a gift another time."

"I'll tell you what you *can* do for me. Get that crazy list. I want to see it and mark off Number 9."

She made a quick run to the bathroom. When she

came back she turned on the lamp, found the list and got a pen. He propped a pillow behind his head. She crawled in next to him and pulled the covers over them both.

He chuckled and snorted a few times as he read.

"Cruise the Amazon River? When do you think you'll ever have a chance to do that?"

"I don't know. Stranger things have happened. Remember this is a list of things for my whole life. Twenty or thirty years from now, who's to say what I might be doing?"

"Star in a movie," he read. "Like that's going to happen."

"You're missing the point."

"Visit Paris in April. That one's probably doable, but *Dance in a ballet?* Are you even a dancer?"

She snatched the list from his hand. "If you're going to make fun of me, you can leave." She tried to get up, but he grabbed her and made her sit down again. He wrapped his arms around her from behind and held her tight against his chest.

"I'm sorry. I didn't mean to hurt your feelings."

"Well, you did."

He kissed her neck, nipped at her ear. "I like the one about growing your pretty hair to your waist, *To tsu hwa.*"

"Call me that again."

"To tsu hwa."

"Talk to me in your language."

The words he spoke were melodious, like a beautiful song.

"What did you say?"

"I said…your smile is brighter than a thousand suns and the blue of your eyes makes the sky weep."

"That's lovely. Did you read it somewhere?"

"No, my heart wrote it."

She sighed and nestled in the curve of his shoulder. "Tell your heart to say some more."

RYAN SHIFTED on the church pew and wished the preacher wasn't so long-winded this morning. The sermon was about sin. Each time he mentioned the word *sinners*, Susannah poked him in the ribs with her elbow. Trying to keep a straight face was becoming impossible.

Covertly, she took something out of her purse, made sure no one was watching and stuffed it in the pocket of his suit pants.

He waited fifteen second, then stuck his hand in and felt. His fingers identified silken panties. He smiled.

"A gift," she whispered. "No need to reciprocate."

AFTER LUNCH, since it was a lovely day, he asked her if she'd like to ride up the Skyway with him and

Nia and look at the mountains. They'd had a light snowfall early that morning, but the sun had since been trying to come out.

Anita had left to go back to school and his mother had other plans. She wanted to take some soup to a sick neighbor. Nana said she was "done going" for the day and preferred to stay home.

"The mountains will be beautiful with the rays hitting the snow and ice," Ryan told Susannah. "How about it?"

"I'd love to go. I can get some photos."

Nia wasn't happy with the decision. She wanted to drive into town and see the Christmas lights that had been turned on the day before.

"We'll do both," he said.

When they'd changed out of their good clothes, Susannah met them at the front door of the barn. Her attitude toward Nia didn't seem any different than the day before and he was glad of that. In minutes Susannah had her giggling as usual.

"We'll head up into the mountains first and then swing through town on the way back," he said. "After that, we'll go see Helen for a minute. That okay with everyone?"

They agreed.

Over the next half hour, they climbed steadily upward along the curving road. Ryan pulled off into one of the scenic overlooks.

"Are all these mountains the Snowbirds?" Susannah asked as they got out of the truck. They walked toward the edge.

"No, but each is part of the Appalachians. The Nantahala Mountains come in from the east and the Unicoi from the west. To the north are the Great Smokies."

"And most of this land is national forest?"

"That's right. The Skyway goes through both the Nantahala and Cherokee National Forests, but we have other forests and wilderness areas, as well. We drove through a different part of the Nantahala when we went down to see Helen last night in Andrews. Remember the steep gorges? You were scared we'd go off the road."

"That was a terrible drive. Worried me to death."

Nia asked, "Were you scared, Susannah?"

"For a minute, but your daddy reminded me that he was familiar with the road and knew what he was doing. So I wasn't scared after that."

"We'll come back through before dark this time. I promise."

Ryan sat on the stone wall while Susannah walked around and took her photos. He warned Nia not to go near the edge, but kept an eye on her. She seemed content to play nearby.

Susannah came back, cheeks rosy and puffing from the high altitude. "I can tell we're high up."

"About 5,300 feet."

"I need to get in better shape. Whew!" She bent over, put her hands on her knees and took a few deep breaths.

He glanced at Nia. She wasn't paying them any attention and was out of earshot. "There's nothing wrong with your shape," he said in a low voice. "And I should know. I've touched every inch of it."

"I have a fondness for your shape, too."

"Enough that you might consider staying around past Christmas?"

She straightened. "Ryan, we talked about this last night. We agreed we'd enjoy what time we have together but not make any promises."

"I'm not asking for a commitment and I'm not prepared to give one, but I *would* like time to build on what we've started. Maybe we'd be good together and maybe we wouldn't, but how are we going to know if you run off?"

"And if I stayed? What then? How would I support myself?"

"Doing what you're doing now, working for me. You like the job, don't you?"

"Yes."

"And you're great at it. In the past month you've already brought me three new clients and convinced that gallery in Atlanta to sell my museum-quality pieces. I should make you my agent. But if you'd rather not work with me, then do whatever you enjoy. You're a great natural photographer. Maybe you could take some classes and learn to do that professionally. Or teach computing. Do bookkeeping. Design and build Web sites. Hell, you have a number of talents you could use to make a living."

"I have other concerns." She nodded toward Nia. "The longer I stay, the harder it'll be on her—and me—if our...relationship doesn't work out."

"Sometimes life is a risk. You know that."

"My body I'm prepared to risk. But my heart...I couldn't go through another break-up. I laugh and call Andrew a jerk, but he *hurt* me."

"I wouldn't hurt you."

"You can't be sure of that. You have the capacity for hurting me even more deeply than he did."

"And why is that?"

"Because my heart's already tender. And because...in the short time we've known each other, I've come to care for you so much it frightens me. I don't *want* to feel this way."

"Susannah..." He stood and drew her closer. "Don't dismiss what you feel. Give us a chance."

"I'm afraid to, Ryan, and not only because of what happened with Andrew. Those years I spent caring for my mother were like being in prison—

worse than prison, because I lived every day with the knowledge that my escape would only come with the death of the person I loved. The guilt and pain were terrible. I don't want to be in the position of feeling that again, of having to take care of someone. I'd rather be alone.''

"I'm not asking you to take care of me or Nia."

"No, but love automatically carries that responsibility."

"Of *helping,* yes, of being a *partner* and a *friend,* but don't you understand that you're supposed to get as much out of a relationship as you give to it?"

"Of course."

"From what you've said, I'm not so sure you do. Was Andrew there when you needed him? Did he understand your pain and help you, or make life more difficult?"

"The break-up wasn't entirely his fault."

"You're not answering me."

"Okay, he wasn't much help. Is that what you want to hear? Having to worry about his feelings on top of everything else put more strain on me. Frankly, he was selfish. He never tried to understand how difficult my life was or to ease my burden."

"I thought so. And your mother drained you, too."

She pulled away. "Now, wait. That was a totally different situation. She was seriously ill and she didn't have anyone else. She was terrified of having to go into a nursing home and being cared for by strangers. I owed it to her to help any way I could.''

''I'm not criticizing you for it, only pointing out that the strong relationships you've had in recent years have both been one-sided, and that's forced you to close off your emotions.'' He pulled her back into his arms and rested his chin on the top of her head. ''I'd like the chance to prove to you that letting someone in doesn't have to be painful, but I can't do that if you're not here. Stay awhile. No pressure, I promise. If you decide you're unhappy and want to leave, I won't make it hard on you.''

''Ryan, you're trying to get me to give up my newfound freedom.''

''No, I'm not, but I know you've been happy here. All I ask is that you be honest about that and consider staying. Think about it some more and don't make a hasty decision.''

''All right.''

Nia came over then and showed him a pretty rock she'd found under the snow. ''Do you think the Little People left it for me?''

''They might have.''

''We need to give them somethin' back.''

He reached in his pocket and got a quarter. ''They like shiny things. Leave this where you found the rock.''

She went back, gingerly placed it on the ground and began looking for more rocks.

"I hope you have a lot of quarters," Susannah said.

AS THEY DROVE down into the valley, she asked him about the various places and how they got their names. Ryan didn't mind. He liked talking about his home and the history of his area.

"Why Snowbird?"

"The old ones say a giant snowbird used to live on top of the tallest mountain," he said. "That's how the range got its name. We call our single mountain Snowbird because we have so many of the birds every winter, but it's only a nickname."

"And why is the community called Sitting Dog?"

"Have you noticed the big outcropping of rock above the house and to the left? Up close it looks like a sitting dog. I'll take you there one day this week. It's only a short walk. I also want to show you something else, near the rock."

They drove to Robbinsville so Nia could see the Christmas lights strung across the streets and those in the store windows.

"We should be getting ours out and putting them up," he told her. "Did you tell Susannah that you're an elf in your ballet recital?"

"I forgot!" Excitedly she gave Susannah every

little detail of her performance. "I wanted to be a deer," she finished, "but Miss Cummings said I had to be an elf. That's what she calls them. They're really Little People, though."

"Oh, that sounds wonderful. Do you get to wear a costume?"

"Uh-huh. A green one. Will you make it for me?"

"Nia, Gran already said she'd do it," Ryan told her.

"But I want Susannah to."

He glanced across the truck at her. "You don't have to, Susannah. My mother already volunteered."

"I don't mind. Actually, I love to sew. I used to do it all the time, but I sold my sewing machine when I sold the house because I didn't think I'd have any use for it."

"You'll probably regret taking on this project."

"Oh, don't spoil my fun." She turned to Nia in the back seat. "Tell you what. I'll make your costume if you'll help me make decorations to hang in the cabin."

"I can do that!"

"Your daddy was telling me how your family celebrates with natural and handmade decorations. We can make colored rings and popcorn balls and stars out of aluminum foil. Stars are okay, aren't they, Ryan?''

"Stars are fine.'' Ryan smiled to himself. She was enjoying this as much as Nia.

"And we can get pinecones from the woods. Let's see what else. Oh, we can dry orange slices and sprinkle them with sugar.''

"Can we eat them?'' Nia asked.

"Eat my decorations?'' She gasped. "Certainly not. Well, maybe a few of them.''

Ryan told her it was fine to collect berries, seed pods, discarded nests, nuts and whatever else she needed from the property but to be careful not to stray too far from the house.

"When? When?'' Nia asked. "Today?''

"Mm, *if* we get back in time. But next Saturday would be better because we'd have all day to gather what we're going to use. And first we'll have to make a list of other things we need, like glue and paper and ribbon. Did your ballet teacher give you any instructions about your costume? We could get the fabric at the same time.''

"Nia brought home a sheet saying when the recital is and what they need,'' Ryan said. "I'll show it to you when we get home.''

THEY VISITED Helen and Maggie at the hospital, then drove home; it was already dark when they arrived.

"You're coming in, aren't you?" Ryan asked.

Susannah decided she wouldn't. He'd want to talk about her staying, and she didn't want to discuss it anymore. What was the point?

"I think I'll take a bath, maybe read a while and go to bed early. And you should spend some time with Nia for a change—without me always hanging around."

He didn't argue. She couldn't tell from his expression what he was thinking or feeling. "I'll see you in the morning then," was his only response.

She told them both good-night and walked over to the cabin with a heavy heart. Why did everything always have to be so complicated?

She'd come here with a simple goal—to take lessons—and now Ryan was asking her to change their entire arrangement. And for what? The *chance* that they *might* be able to build a lasting relationship. No, thanks. She'd been through that once and she never intended to open herself up to that kind of pain again.

Even if she did stay and things worked out, he had a sick daughter who needed special attention and—fond as she was of Nia—Susannah had spent nearly a third of her life in the role of caregiver. She didn't need, didn't want, that responsibility again.

Once inside, she turned up the heat, filled the tub and had a long, leisurely soak. The warm water soothed her body but not her troubled mind.

She looked around the cabin at all the little improvements she'd made—the throw rug, the pillows for the couch, the Kiss the Cook spoon holder for the kitchen—and realized she'd turned it into a home, a foolish thing to do.

And why on earth had she asked Nia to help her decorate when she wouldn't even be here for Christmas? She'd be on the road somewhere between North Carolina and New York.

She'd gotten caught up in the idea of having a true Christmas again, been reminded of her own childhood when she and her mother had decorated the house. But she *wasn't* Nia's mother. Best to remember that for the child's sake and her own.

A hard knock sounded. She grabbed her towel.

"Who is it?"

"It's me," Ryan said.

"Are you alone?"

"Yes."

Susannah relaxed and tossed the towel onto the floor. "Come in."

He opened the door, then stopped abruptly and stared.

"Well, come in or get out, for goodness' sake.

I'm freezing to death!'' She settled back and sponged bubbles over her arm.

He closed the door and walked toward her.

"Where's Nia?" she asked.

"I took her to Mother's for a little while."

"Why?"

"Because I wanted to be with you."

"You've been with me all day. Go home, Ryan. I'm taking a bath."

"You seem to be having a good time."

"I'm having a wonderful time."

He bent over and pulled off one boot, then the second one. He started on his shirt.

"What are you *doing?*"

"What does it look like I'm doing? I'm getting in there with you."

"Oh, no, you're not. Ryan!" She giggled as he hastily stripped down to nothing. He got in, sloshing water everywhere. "Look at the mess you've made all over the floor."

"I'll mop it up."

"And you've soaked my cast."

"It's about to come off anyway."

His big body had displaced so much water it was still spilling over the rim.

He grabbed her around the waist and pulled her forward, maneuvering them both until she was sitting between his legs.

"Growing up, I once asked my father why mother had insisted on having such a big bathtub in here and he just grinned. Now I know why." He took her sponge away and began using it to wash her shoulders and breasts.

"You felt bad when he didn't call on Thanksgiving, didn't you? I overheard you saying something to your mother."

"He could at least have bothered to pick up the phone."

"Has it been hard for you, being the oldest and feeling responsible for everyone? I know you're paying Anita's tuition and I've seen you slip money to Joe more than once."

"Sometimes it's hard. But being a part of this family means I have obligations, and not only financial ones. But it's the same with each of us. My brothers and sister, Mom, Nana—they've been my strength. I hope, in return, I've been theirs."

"You're a nice man. Do you know that?"

"I know," he teased. "I'm special."

Susannah laughed. "And modest."

"I also have some very selective skills."

"Oh? And tell me, what might those be?"

He picked her up and sat her down on his lap so that her legs hooked behind him and their most intimate places touched. "I'd rather show you."

CHAPTER TEN

THE FOLLOWING Tuesday Susannah went with Ryan to the community center to begin assembling the mosaic. Joe came to help and brought a digital video camera.

"Nice equipment," Susannah said, admiring it. Very high-end. Expensive. She looked through the viewfinder and tinkered with all the controls. "Brand-new?"

"Yep."

"Hooks into a TV or computer?"

"Right."

"I'm so jealous. Must've cost you a fortune."

"Hey, not me. Ryan paid for it."

Ryan jumped in and said he wanted to have a video record of the mural.

"What a great idea," Susannah told him. "You should do that with all your commissions, start to finish. Video the work while it's in progress and the final product and make a compact disc. You'd have a terrific sales tool, much better than the still photographs we've been mailing out."

"Pretty much what I had in mind *if* I can learn to work the stupid thing."

Joe had used a friend's before, so he spent five minutes showing them both what to do.

"Simple," he said, finishing. "Not too different from Susannah's camera."

"Looks pretty simple," Ryan agreed, "even for me."

They began installing the panels, putting in both a water-resistant and a soundproof membrane and then attaching the cement backerboard to the wall studs. At intervals, Joe took video of Ryan at work with Susannah helping.

Because this room would be used primarily for a day care center and the walls would take a lot of abuse, Ryan had used vitreous tile fired for thirty-plus hours at twenty-two hundred degrees.

Joints cleverly hidden in the design would allow the materials to expand and contract without damage.

Vitreous, impervious…Susannah had picked up the terminology and actually understood what it meant. She knew the difference between an edging and a margin trowel. The array of adhesives still confused her, but she was pleased with what she'd learned.

Ryan looked around and said they were making

excellent progress. Completing the work wouldn't take many more days.

He'd finished tiling every panel, with the exception of the one that held the caricatures of his own family. That one he'd been working on after hours and hadn't brought down from the workshop.

"When are you going to let me have a peek?" Susannah asked.

"I'm not."

"How come?"

"Because the only reward I get from a donated project like this is people's reaction. If you or Joe or anybody else knows what it all looks like, you won't be surprised. That spoils it for me. So I'm holding something back. You'll have to wait for the dedication."

"Makes sense," Joe said.

She pinched him on the arm.

"Ouch!"

"You're supposed to side with me, you traitor."

"Joe's going to help me install the panel because it's too heavy to do alone. Once it's up, I'll lay in the tile on the missing part. Then we'll be ready for the unveiling."

"How have you portrayed your mother and grandmother?"

"You'll have to wait and see."

"No hints even?"

''All I'll tell you is that your birds are going in there.''

She smiled delightedly. One day he'd supervised as she'd created a pair of snowbirds out of the tiniest tiles, but she'd assumed the piece was only for practice and not of any importance.

''Oh, Ryan, seriously? You're going to use my birds?''

When he nodded, she was so excited, she kissed both him and Joe, then danced around.

Joe grabbed the video camera and recorded her craziness.

She didn't care. She had created something artistic and beautiful! *Her!* Susannah Pelton. And for years and years people would enjoy her work.

This was so much better than just assisting with the background pieces. She'd only been following Ryan's design and pattern then. The birds were *her* idea, her creation. Even Ryan had said she'd done a great job.

''Where are they going exactly?'' she asked.

''I'm not telling.''

She begged for details, but he wouldn't give in. If Joe hadn't been there, she probably could have convinced him to tell, but she had to behave. Joe was already suspicious of them. He'd been sending them sly grins all afternoon.

Ryan had gently patted her bottom when she

kissed him and the intimacy of that hadn't escaped Joe's notice. He'd winked at her over Ryan's shoulder.

She had a hard time settling down. Twice Ryan told her to stop singing because it was driving him crazy.

"Okay, Mr. Grinch."

Late in the afternoon, Ryan looked at his watch and commented that it was nearly time for Nia's bus to arrive.

"How about picking her up and staying through her ballet lesson?" he asked Susannah. "You can watch the kids practice for their recital. Joe and I can handle things here."

"Yeah, get lost," Joe suggested. "We need some peace and quiet."

"I get the impression you don't like my singing."

"That's putting it mildly," Ryan said, making Joe snicker.

She said she'd go. She needed to talk to Nia's teacher, anyway, about her costume for the dance.

On her way out, she launched into a loud chorus of "Respect." Joe got it all on video, including Ryan covering his ears.

RYAN WAITED until he was certain Susannah had left the room, then asked Joe if he thought she'd suspected.

"Didn't seem to."

"I appreciate your helping me pull this off. You sure you can find someone to put together what I want?"

"Positive. All we have to do is get enough video of her to have a good selection. I know a guy who can do the editing."

"Perfect. What about the other? Did you have any problems getting Sandy to agree?"

"No, she's glad to do it."

"More likely glad to do *you* a favor."

"Things aren't like that between us."

"You've never dated her? I thought you had. She's had a crush on you since first grade."

"Nah, she's a good kid. I like her too much. I don't date women I like."

"Run that by me again."

"I date for fun and for, you know…"

"To get laid."

"Yeah, but once I've been in a woman's bed a few times, she starts getting clingy and I have to break it off. If it's someone I like or I've grown up with, it wrecks the friendship."

"You have a strange way of handling women."

"Look who's talking! You say you care about Susannah and want her to stay, yet you're helping her fulfill her fantasies and go off without you. I don't get it."

"Do you remember the story about eagle and mouse? One of the elders told it last summer at the powwow."

"No, I sneaked off to swap body fluids with Willow Silverfox."

"I should've guessed. Anyway…the point of the story was that sometimes the best way to hold on is to let go."

"Damn, Ryan, I swear half the time I don't understand you. You're sounding more like Nana Sipsey every day."

"I'll take that as a great compliment, brother."

SHE LOVED WATCHING the girls dance. A couple of times Susannah had picked Nia up on Tuesday and come early enough to sit through class.

The dance performance was about the mother spirit of earth who gives presents to good children. Afterward, small boxes of sugar cookies would be handed out by the girls to each family.

In a way, it was the Santa Claus legend, but the young teacher had wisely incorporated the beliefs of the Cherokee. Both whites and Indians should enjoy the performance.

Nia and her friends Iva and Mary were elves, or rather Little People. The other five girls would be sacred deer or reindeer, however you wanted to look at it.

Nia seemed to love her class. Susannah suspected it was because this was one of the few times she saw her friends outside of school.

She'd only go to Mary's or Iva's if Ryan stayed with her, and that had become a problem. The girls had noticed Nia's reluctance to be separated from her father. They'd begun to tease her.

"My shoes, please," she said from the metal chair beside her. She stuck her tiny feet in Susannah's lap for help in putting on her ballet slippers.

"How did things go today?" Susannah asked.

Nia obviously knew what she meant: had the girls said anything hurtful?

"Mary called me a name."

"What did she say?"

"She's not gonna invite me to her house anymore. She said I don't come 'cause I'm a baby."

"And what did you tell her?"

"That I didn't want to go to her stupid house, anyway."

Nia glanced over at the girls, sitting on the floor putting on their ballet shoes. Mary looked at Nia and whispered something to Iva. They both giggled.

"They don't like me anymore," Nia said, crestfallen.

"Oh, I'm sure that's not true. Go over there and talk to them. Act like nothing's happened."

"Can I wear your magic ring? Please, please? I promise I'll give it back after class."

"You understand, don't you, that this ring isn't really magic? What makes it special is that it was given to me by someone who loved me very much. Her *love*—not the ring—is what gave me the courage not to be afraid."

"Okay, but can I please wear it?"

Susannah wasn't sure her lecture had made an impact. Nia was six and scared. Like every child, she craved belief in a protector, even if it came in the form of a magic ring.

"All right, this one time, but be very careful. My mother gave it to me when I was six or seven, I've kept it all these years." Susannah took the ring from the chain. "Don't lose it."

"I won't." Nia slipped it on her finger.

She hopped down and kissed her, then scurried off to face her friends.

The sweet gesture touched Susannah. Tears formed, but she quickly got herself under control. Crying here in public would be embarrassing. Several of the mothers had stayed to watch their daughters rehearse.

Sandy Cummings, the young teacher, waved at her from across the room and walked over.

"I'm glad to see you here today. I wanted to ask a favor."

"Sure."

"I was wondering if you'd consider being our mother spirit for the recital. I'm doing the narration, so I'd planned to ask one of the parents to play the role."

"Sandy, I'm not Nia's parent, only a friend of the family."

"I know, but that doesn't matter. You've shown an interest in the class, and you're about my size so we could easily make you a costume from one of my old leotards."

She leaned over and whispered that some of the mothers were a bit too hefty to consider putting into stretch fabric.

"I'm not sure about this," Susannah said.

"The dance you'd do isn't hard. A few twirls. Some basic movements. I could teach you in thirty minutes if you could stay after class."

"You mean I'd actually dance? I thought you wanted me to pass out gift boxes to the elves or something."

"Well, of course you'd dance. Please, Susannah. You'd be perfect."

Imagining the mothers and fathers staring at her made gooseflesh appear on her arms. How silly she'd look out there on the floor, flitting around with the kids.

But so what? Dancing in a ballet *was* on her list.

"I'll do it."

"AND RIGHT HERE I jump and make a turn." Susannah demonstrated for them in the living room of his mother's house. "And then I bow gracefully."

"Yay!" Nia cheered.

"Lovely, Susannah!" his mother said.

Nana clapped and said it was wonderful. *"Do yu yo go os da!"*

Ryan put down the video camera and clapped, too. "You'll do a great job."

"I hope so. I wouldn't want to mess up and ruin the performance."

"I doubt you could do that. Sa Sa, your turn. Dance for Gran and Nana and I'll record it."

Like Susannah, she got up and went through her part.

"Now you and Susannah together."

They dipped and glided, a couple of times nearly bumping into each other, making everyone laugh.

"We're good, aren't we, Daddy?" Nia asked.

"You sure are. I've never seen anything prettier."

"Of course we don't have our music," Susannah

pointed out. "We'd be much better, wouldn't we, Nia?"

"Uh-huh. A hundred times better."

"I'm not sure I could stand you being any better," Ryan told them.

They wanted to show him a second time. After both had gone through their routines, Susannah hooked the camera to the TV and they watched the replay.

"Show it again," Nia said.

"No, that's enough for one night. Time for us to head home."

"Not yet. Please?"

"'Dexter's Laboratory' comes on in twenty minutes. You don't want to miss that."

"Can't I watch it here?"

"No, we need to go. Daddy wants to work later tonight."

Susannah said she could bring her home after the TV show was over, that she wanted to stay a little longer, too, and visit with his mother and grandmother.

"Why don't you let Nia spend the night with me at the cabin?" she said. "I can take her to school in the morning, since I've got to go to town anyway and have my cast removed. Nia, would you like to come home with me? We could make popcorn and play Go Fish.''

"Our own sleep-over?" she asked. Ryan could tell by her voice she was interested but hesitant.

"That's right. Except that your daddy would be close by, just across the driveway.''

Nia bit her lip and thought about it.

Ryan pulled Susannah aside. He wasn't sure this was a good idea and he told her so. "I've explained what can happen.''

"Ryan, this is a perfect chance for her to be away from you, but not so far that she gets upset. She does okay when she stays here with your mother, doesn't she?''

"Most of the time. Sometimes she cries and wants to come home, but not very often. She's used to Mom and Nana. But that doesn't mean she *won't* have an anxiety attack and they're scary as hell.''

"Give me your cell phone. That way I can reach you, and she'll be able to call if she feels homesick or afraid.''

"She'd probably end up not staying the night.''

"If she doesn't, that's okay. Let her try.''

"I *worry* she'll get sick.''

"Ryan, her friends are starting to make fun of her. Do you realize that?''

"She told you they have?''

"I've seen them. And she's miserable because of it. They don't want to invite her over anymore and they've stopped coming here. Do you want her to become even more isolated than she already is?"

"No."

"Then let her spend the night with me."

He had reservations, but hell, she was right. Nia had to learn that she could be separated from him and nothing bad would happen. Susannah was trustworthy. And he'd be two minutes away if they needed him.

"She has to *want* to go," he stipulated.

"Help me convince her."

THE WOMEN had moved to the kitchen for a cup of tea, but they could see Nia through the doorway watching her program. Ryan had left to work for a few hours.

"Do you think she'll come?" Susannah asked Ryan's mother.

"If not this night, then another."

"I don't have too many more nights left here. I hate to leave Sitting Dog not knowing if she's going to be okay."

"Then stay," Annie suggested. "You're welcome to live in the cabin as long as you'd like."

"I appreciate that, but I've already made plans to drive to New York around Christmas."

"Plans can be changed. Is what's in New York so important?"

"Yes. Well, no. It's hard to explain."

Granted, the event itself wasn't that important. They'd been dropping the ball on New Year's Eve for years and would probably continue to do it for many more. But being able to see it represented the freedom Susannah had gained upon her mother's death, the freedom she wanted to protect.

Maybe that was being shallow and self-serving, but she feared the outcome if she changed her plans. That one concession might lead to another, then another, and pretty soon she'd be right back where she'd been originally, catering to the needs and desires of someone else.

"My leaving doesn't mean I don't care about Nia's welfare," she told Annie. "Please understand that."

"I do. Don't fret about it. Ryan explained about your mother and your role in looking after her."

"Nia means a great deal to me, and I'm worried about her."

Nana Sipsey nodded and said something in Cherokee mixed with English. Susannah only understood a little bit. *Heart* was one of the words. And something about many children.

"I didn't get all of that. What about children?"

"She says you worry because the child is already in your heart," Ryan's mother said. "But there's no need for concern. Nia will be happy again. Nana has burned the sacred tobacco. In the smoke she's seen the child surrounded by many others she'll call brother and sister, including two little ones with identical faces."

"She has visions?"

"Glimpses of what will come. I've never known her to be wrong."

Susannah swallowed hard. She wanted Nia to be well, but she hated imagining Ryan married and creating lots of babies with some other woman.

"No disrespect to Nana, but I'm not sure I believe in such things."

"You're young. In time, the truth will find you."

NIA DECIDED she *would* spend the night. They stopped by the barn, packed a suitcase with clothes and everything else she thought she'd need, which turned out to be enough that Ryan had to drive them over in the truck.

Dolls, toys, books… She even insisted on taking the cat, which meant they also had to make sure they brought her food and rigged up a temporary litter box.

Ryan found a discarded plant tray that would do if he taped over the drainage holes in the bottom.

They got everything inside the cabin and an area for Abigail squared away. Susannah warned him not to linger or make a fuss.

"Act like this is no big deal and Nia will, too."

"I'll try."

"'Night, you two," he called out. "Have fun."

"We will," Susannah said cheerily.

Nia was busy unpacking the ten million games she'd brought. She stopped and turned. "Daddy?"

Susannah held her breath. Beside her, Ryan had stiffened.

"Yes, goosey?"

"You forgot my kiss."

They both exhaled.

"You're right, I did. Come here."

She ran to him and he kissed her on the forehead.

"Now give one to Susannah."

Ryan gave Susannah a kiss on the forehead, too. His look said he'd like to give her a much better one and on the mouth.

"Rain check," she murmured.

He left quickly as promised. Susannah, determined to make this work, suggested she and Nia first take their baths and get into their pajamas.

"Then we won't have to worry about doing that when we're sleepy and ready to go to bed."

Nia took her bath, then Susannah. They had a tea party with apple juice and popcorn and played some of the child's favorite games.

As her bedtime approached, Nia got more restless. Twice she went to the window and looked across to the barn.

"Will Daddy be unhappy without me?" she asked.

"He'll be fine. He's not far. See his light? If he's feeling sad, he can walk over."

"And I can walk over there?"

"You could, but it would be such a nice present if we left him alone to work. He very much wants to finish the mosaic he's doing for the center."

"But if I get scared I can call him?"

"Of course you can. We'll put the phone right here—" she set it on the corner of the table "—where you can see it from the bed. And we'll leave a light on. Okay?"

"Are you gonna sleep with me?"

"I sure am. I'm really tired." She wasn't, but if her lying down made Nia feel better, she would.

They brushed their teeth and used the bathroom.

Nia said her prayers; noticeably absent was any mention of her mother, which Susannah thought strange.

They climbed into bed. Abigail immediately jumped up and settled at Susannah's feet. Cooper the bear lay tucked between them.

"Was Mary nicer to you at ballet? I saw all you girls giggling over something."

"She called me a baby. I told her she was an old poop head."

"That's one way to handle it."

"Iva laughed and then I did and then Mary did."

"Sounds like you're friends again. Sometimes kids say mean things to each other, but it's best to make up and not let it bother you."

"Did kids call you names when you was little?"

"Sometimes. One little boy used to call me 'carrot head' all the time."

"Did you get mad?"

"A little bit, but he was silly and I told him so."

She thought Nia would close her eyes then and go to sleep, but she wanted to talk a while. She told her about the other kids at school, the ones she liked and didn't and about one named Woody who put a snail on her milk carton.

"Boys are weird."

Susannah had to agree.

Nia yawned and rolled in her direction, resting her head on Susannah's shoulder. Once during the night she cried out, but didn't wake. Susannah held her close and rubbed her back.

Nana was right. This child was in her heart. And she would miss her terribly.

CHAPTER ELEVEN

RYAN PUT THE FOOD in his backpack and added two bottles of water. What else did they need? The video camera. He hurried to get it.

Susannah saw the bath towels he'd laid out and wrinkled her nose. "Why are we taking these?"

"So we can dry off at the pool."

"*Dry off?* Ryan, it's thirty-five degrees outside! We can't go swimming in this cold!"

"Where we're going it's warm."

"In the middle of the woods?"

"Yep." He wriggled his eyebrows. "And bathing suits are optional."

"This place isn't too far, is it?"

"Only forty-five minutes or so."

"Couldn't we do something a little less...outdoorsy?"

"You'll love this. I promise."

"A picnic in the snow and a dip in a pond in December?"

"That's right."

"Okay." She threw up her hands. "If you're willing, so am I."

Climbing the mountain, she kept up better than he'd thought she would and didn't complain. Not too much, anyway. A couple of times he stopped and took video of the scenery, always careful to include her.

"I understand why you're in such good shape," she said, resting a moment with her hands on her waist. "This kind of activity definitely keeps you slim."

"We're lucky the snow's almost melted. Let me know when you need a break and we'll stop."

"I'm fine. Don't get too far ahead, though. I have no idea where we are."

A while later he called a halt and they shared some of the water. He pulled her woolen cap down further on her ears.

"We're almost there."

They were playing hooky today, celebrating three things: Nia's staying at the cabin all night, Ryan's finishing the last of the tiling for the mosaic and Susannah's getting the cast off her wrist.

Nia was in school, and that meant he and Susannah could be alone for a little while. He also wanted to show her several places that were special to him.

First they went to the outcropping of rock that had given the community its name.

"Oh, gosh, it *does* look like a sitting dog," Susannah said. "And from below I never would've guessed how big it is."

"Estimating size is hard in the woods. What looks ten feet tall from far away can be a hundred feet when you get close. Same with distance. You can think you're a mile from something and you're really twenty miles."

"How tall would you guess the dog is? Sixty feet?"

"She's that easily."

"She? Rocks are females?"

"Grandfather said when he was a little boy *his* grandfather told him the legend of this place. Want to hear it?"

"You know I do."

"A wild dog—a wolf—disappeared during a hunt. His mate sat here waiting for him to return, but days and nights passed, then more days and nights. Obviously he'd been killed, but she wouldn't accept it. She said he'd only lost his way and she'd guide him home with her voice. Her long, forlorn howls could be heard with each rising of the moon. She died, looking out across the mountains, still waiting for the one she loved to come back to her. The spirit of the wind was so impressed with her devotion that it turned her into a large stone. Now she's a guide to all who might lose their way and the wind still carries her nightly cries.''

''That's one of your sadder stories.''

''I don't make them up. I only tell them.''

She breathed in the air. ''This is a lovely place. So quiet.''

''Grandfather bought it years ago to preserve where his ancestors hid out during the removal. When he died, he left this part of the mountain to me. He said I was the only one in the family who truly appreciated it as much as he did.''

''Your grandmother didn't mind?''

''No, she says we're all simply guests of the land, anyway.''

They climbed out onto one of the rock's ledges and ate the cheese and bread he'd brought. After, he took her to the cave, a ten-minute hike. He crawled inside and helped her through the passage.

''Wait a minute while I get us some light.'' He struck a match and lit a kerosene lamp, then the torches in the wall holders.

''Oh!'' Susannah walked around in amazement.

''My ancestors lived here for more than two years. I still have pieces of some of the skins they used and the arrow points. Come see this.'' He showed her the crudely drawn pictures and the hand-prints. ''Here's the one for *Numma hi tsune ga*. His father's. My grandfather's. My father's. This is mine.''

"*Siquutsets,*" she read below it.

"My Indian name. Possum. Grandfather said as a baby I'd eat anything that didn't try to eat me first."

That made her chuckle. "I can believe that. I've seen you eat."

"He was of the *Ani Wahwa,* the wolf clan, once known as the warriors of the tribe. Long ago, members of a clan were like families and forbidden to marry each other. Most Cherokee don't know their clan affiliations today, but Grandfather still believed in the old ways. And even though he loved a girl, he wouldn't marry her because she was *Ani Wahwa.* He made a match with a stranger, a girl of the *Ani Wodi.* Her ancestors had made the red paint for war and religious ceremonies. They were also known for their ability to heal."

"So he and your grandmother didn't love each other when they got married?"

"No, but they came to in time."

"I'm glad about that. I'd hate to think Nana had a loveless marriage."

He took down the jar of dried ground clay and dipped his fingers in the dust.

"She says red is the color of a woman's power. Her ability to create life makes her superior to a man."

"I doubt many men would agree. Do you? Are women superior because they can give birth?"

"I believe a woman's ability to conceive makes her *special*. Neither sex is superior."

"A diplomatic answer."

"No, I'm being honest. Men and women have different strengths. Where one is weak, the other is strong. We were created that way on purpose. Conception may be a miracle, but the act that brings it about is commonplace, so I'd argue that the willingness to raise a child after its birth is more important than either conception or delivery."

"I agree with that."

He showed her the rest of the cave, the back room, the little basin of water suitable for washing utensils but not to drink.

"I keep a few supplies and wood for a fire," he explained. "I come here when I need to clear my head."

"You spend the night?"

"Sometimes. As a boy I spent a lot of nights here."

"Alone?" She shivered as if she had a chill. "I don't think I'd be brave enough for that."

"I always believed the souls of my ancestors watched over me."

Her eyes widened, and she glanced about with trepidation.

"They aren't here right now, are they?"

He laughed loudly, his voice echoing off the rock.

THE CREEK was high due to runoff from all the snowfall, and Susannah seemed nervous at crossing the narrow log bridge.

"I should admit I don't swim well, hardly at all. If I fall in, don't expect me to be able to save myself."

Ryan took her hand. "We'll cross together. I only see one icy patch. Step over it."

Despite her uneasiness, she went ahead, and they made it to the other side without incident. Upstream they climbed through rocks pushed to the surface by recent volcanic activity, "recent" meaning a few hundred thousand years ago.

The hot springs was another of his secret places, thirty minutes from the cave. Not even his siblings knew about this spot. Susannah laughed with delight when she saw the series of pools, steam rising from their surfaces.

"We can go in? The water isn't too hot?"

"The temperature's usually perfect, but since the water's heated by vents in the earth and they can be unpredictable, I'm careful to check first before I go in."

"Which should we try?"

"That one has the best depth for sitting and relaxing. The thermometer on the post over here tells me it's safe.''

They stayed in the pool for more than an hour, splashing, soaking, making love.

''Do you suppose your great-great-whatever-grandparents played like this?'' she asked, settling against his side.

''Probably.''

''I feel like I'm in our own little Garden of Eden.''

''Isn't this better than Paris?''

''Mm...different.'' She rubbed her hand across his naked chest and down his stomach to his groin. He inhaled as she teased him with her fingers.

''What has Paris got that my mountain doesn't?''

''The Eiffel Tower, cafés that serve real French onion soup, the River Seine...''

''Are those things really so important?''

''They are if you've never experienced them. I want to see and do everything I can while I'm still young enough.''

''So you keep reminding me.''

He climbed out of the pool, his joy in the day tarnished.

''Ryan?''

''Time to leave.''

''Are you mad at me?''

''Not mad. Disappointed.'' He grabbed a towel

and hastily began to dry off before the cold air chilled him.

She followed him out and sought her own towel.

"I don't understand why you're hell-bent on running all over the world when the best it has to offer you is right here," he said. "It's crazy."

"That's not fair! You've seen this world you say isn't as special as your mountain. I haven't. You get to fly places and visit clients all the time."

"Not anymore."

"But you used to before Nia got sick, and you will again when she's well. Plus, you've been to other countries. All I've ever done is drive through a few states."

They quickly hopped into their clothes.

"That's a minor problem. I could take you with me when I travel on business and we'll plan vacations anywhere you want to go."

"That sounds very much like a commitment."

"Maybe it is."

"Only a few days ago you weren't ready for one."

"Things can change in a few days."

"We hardly know each other."

"I know enough about you to be certain I don't want you walking out of my life in three weeks." He took a breath and tried to calm down. "Stay longer. Give us…six months. If you're not happy at the end of it and still want to go, I'll help you pack.''

"Ryan, I…'' She shook her head. "I'm not ready for this. It's too soon.''

He clasped her by the shoulders. "You're scared. I understand that. The last few years have been tough for you. But you can't keep running away from life.''

"I'm not. I'm *embracing* life.''

"Are you? How? By jumping off bridges? Susannah, real life isn't an adrenaline rush. It's ballet lessons…and playing the tooth fairy… It's sitting up with your spouse after the kids have gone to bed to talk about each other's day. Don't you want that? Don't you want to be part of a family again, to love and be loved?''

"Yes, someday. Maybe.''

He let his hands drop. "Maybe?''

"The pain of Andrew's desertion and the memories of what I had to endure during my mother's illness are still too fresh for me to know what I want. That's my whole reason for traveling and seeing new things. Until my mother died I'd hardly ever been out of Georgia. My only experience living on my own had been the year away at college, and that was in the next state. You have a strong sense of who you are and what your place is on this planet. Who am I? What's my place?''

"I can't answer that for you."

"Which is my point. You're asking me to choose a life that might not be the right one for me."

"You won't know if it's right until you give it a fair chance."

"I won't know it's right until I see what else is out there."

"Do you hear yourself? You're talking about love by default, of settling for it only if you can't find something more exciting. Well, sorry, sweetheart, that's not the way it works. And I don't buy your flimsy excuse for running off. If you're really free, then you can decide to stay just as much as you can decide to go. You're letting that stupid list dictate what you do, and that's worse than being confused about what you want and who you are."

Fully dressed, he jerked up the backpack and headed out. She fell in behind him.

"I'm sorry," she said. "I don't want to hurt you."

"You're too damn late."

THEY WORKED in near silence the rest of the afternoon. Susannah felt miserable. Ryan would hardly look at her. He only spoke when she asked him a question.

She tried to apologize again, but he refused to discuss the issue anymore.

"I have work to do in back," he finally said, picking up a hammer and leaving.

Susannah slumped in the chair. What had started out as a lovely day was ruined and she didn't know how to fix it. She didn't want Ryan mad at her, but she also wasn't going to lie to him. Why did he have to push so hard? He was asking too much of her.

Clearly it would be best for both of them if she simply left, but how could she when she'd made promises she couldn't break?

Ryan expected her to join the family for the Winter Solstice celebration on December 22. Then there was the center dedication and community party on Christmas Eve when he'd unveil the mosaic. She didn't want to miss that.

Nia would be heartbroken if she didn't attend the ballet recital on the eighteenth or sew that costume. And Sandy Cummings was counting on her participation.

She also had to complete the basket she'd volunteered to make for the arts cooperative. And she couldn't leave without first making Christmas presents for the family.

Okay, she'd have to stick it out until the morning of December 25. Picking up the calendar, she counted the days. Twenty-one. Christmas was just three weeks from today.

She'd take the advice she'd given Nia yesterday

and act as if nothing had happened. Ryan couldn't stay mad at her forever.

He banged away with his hammer all afternoon, occasionally coming in to pick up tiles but not speaking even once.

When it was time to leave, Susannah walked to the door and poked her head inside. He was pounding at a stack of tile he'd wrapped in a sheet, breaking them into random pieces.

He noticed her and took off his safety glasses.

"What?"

"Nia wanted me to get her today so we could buy the material for her costume. Is that okay with you?"

"Fine."

"Are the three of us still going over to Bass and Helen's later?" Helen had come home from the hospital the day before with baby Maggie, and Nia wanted to see her. She'd been too young to go upstairs the night they'd driven to the hospital.

"If you still want to," Ryan said.

"I do. How about if I pick up some chicken on the way back? We can take it with us. I'll get enough for Helen and Bass."

"That's fine." He put down his hammer and reached for his wallet.

"I'll pay for it."

"No, you won't." He came to the door and tried to hand her several bills.

"I said I'll get it."

"Take the money."

"No, I've got money."

They argued back and forth until he shook his head. "Damn, you can be downright stubborn at times," he said, a hint of a smile on his lips.

"No more than you."

"Will you take the damn money?"

"Only if you give me a kiss and tell me you don't hate me."

"You know I don't hate you, Susannah. I wouldn't be so pissed off if I hated you. That's my problem."

"Ryan, please don't be mad. We have so little time left together. I can't bear the thought of us spending it arguing."

He sighed deeply and nodded. "You're right. I'm sorry I lost my temper."

"And I'm sorry I made you lose it. Can we please not fight about this?"

"Come here." He took hold of her shirt and pulled her into his arms. He kissed her deeply and lovingly. "I want you to be happy. Go wherever you feel you have to. See all those places you've dreamed about. I promise I won't try to make you stay."

"Thank you."

She should've been glad, but for some reason she felt even more miserable than before.

THE BABY WAS as cute as Susannah remembered and Helen seemed to be recovering well.

Nia found the infant fascinating. She'd been warned by her daddy not to touch it, but that didn't stop her from standing by the bassinet and gazing at Maggie with wonder while she slept.

She drove Helen crazy asking questions. What did she eat? Why were her fingernails so little? Why did she have a bandage on her belly button? Did she have a boo boo?

Bass teased her and said they'd found Maggie growing in a pumpkin patch. The place on her stomach was where she'd been attached to the plant.

As if she'd been slapped, Nia burst into tears and ran to Ryan, crawling into his lap for consolation.

"Hey, what is it?" Nia didn't answer, only sobbed harder. Susannah tried to comfort her. She pushed her hand away.

"Honestly, Bass," Helen scolded. "Did you have to upset the child?"

"What did I say?"

Their voices and Nia's crying woke the baby. Helen picked her up and walked about, trying to soothe her.

"Nia, honey," she said gently, pacing back and forth, "Uncle Bass was only teasing. Maggie didn't grow on a pumpkin. You remember me showing you my big tummy and telling you the baby was inside?"

Her cries dwindled to sniffles.

"You put your hand there and felt the baby moving around. Remember?"

Nia nodded hesitantly.

"Hey, kiddo, I'm sorry," Bass told her. "I didn't mean to make you cry. I was only playing with you. We didn't find Maggie. Helen and I made her."

"How?" Nia wanted to know.

"Uh, with sugar and spice and everything nice."

"Will she melt?" Her bottom lip trembled.

"Oh, Bass," Helen said, clearly exasperated. She told Nia, "With love, honey. Bass and I made Maggie with love. And that means she'll always be here."

The baby finally stopped crying and immediately began rooting for a nipple.

"She's hungry," Helen said. "Let me go feed her and put her to bed."

Susannah and Ryan stayed another hour and then came home and put Nia to bed, as well. She'd been strangely subdued since her crying spell.

"That was all a bit unnerving," Susannah said when she'd fallen asleep and Ryan had returned to the den. "Why would Bass's joke have gotten her so upset?"

"She told me it wasn't right for people to take babies away. I think she believed they'd found Maggie and decided to keep her."

"I guess when you're six, childbirth is a confusing concept."

"No kidding. You should've heard her asking me questions about how Bass and Helen made the baby."

"What did you tell her?"

"I more or less repeated what Helen said, that sometimes a man and woman can love each other so much that a baby is the result."

"That satisfied her?"

"Yeah, except she turned around and asked me if I'd loved her mother, which threw me for a loop. I didn't know what to say. I'd just told her babies were conceived with love so I didn't want her to think she *wasn't*."

"How did you handle it?"

"I told her I loved her mother in my own way."

"You did the right thing. She was looking for reassurance and you gave it to her, but you didn't lie."

"When she's older, she'll understand my relationship with Carla better. Hell, when I'm older maybe I will, too."

"What do you mean?"

"Nothing. I'm tired and talking crazy. I worked too late last night."

He stretched out on the couch on his stomach and laid his head on her thigh. She rubbed his back while he talked to her, telling about the first time he'd seen Nia.

"She was ugly as sin. Blotchy red. No hair whatsoever."

"And you loved her on sight."

"Yeah, I did. Amazing, isn't it, how something so tiny can have so much power over you? Until I brought Nia home, I didn't realize how much I could love someone. I mean, I love my mother and my family, but when it's your kid... Hell, listen to me. I sound like some old sap."

"I don't think so. There's something incredibly sexy about a man who can have so much devotion to a child."

She ran her fingers through his luxurious hair.

"Mm, that feels good." He yawned twice in rapid succession.

A few minutes later, his breathing deepened and he dropped off to sleep. Susannah didn't disturb him but continued to touch his back and head, enjoying the intimacy of it.

This was what he'd meant by "real" life, a man and woman talking at the end of the day, taking comfort in being with each other, sharing both the good and bad. She had to admit it was nice.

She looked up. Nia stood in the doorway.

"I wet my bed," she said.

Susannah sighed to herself.

This, too, was real life.

CHAPTER TWELVE

IF TIME WAS a constant thing, Susannah wondered why it suddenly seemed to move so swiftly.

When she was a child, the days leading up to Christmas had passed with excruciating slowness. She'd counted them off and dreamed of Santa coming and what he'd leave under the tree. But now they raced by. Two weeks felt like two days.

The flurry of activity was one reason. She hardly had time to breathe. The Whitepaths went all out in celebrating Christmas and the Winter Solstice.

Decorations, entertaining friends, preparing their handmade presents—every moment brought something else to do, including many unusual things she'd never experienced before.

She enjoyed creating the "wishing tree" with its bits of paper in the shape of leaves on which everyone wrote their wishes. *Peace,* she'd written on her leaf, but secretly she'd been more selfish and wished for happiness.

One night the community held a giveaway, where

each family brought a gift and people competed for them with songs, dances and games.

Susannah had never been much of a baker. The best she could do was a store-bought brownie mix now and then. So she didn't volunteer to help with the numerous cakes, breads and desserts the women prepared, but she did have a knack for creating something out of nothing.

With Nia's eager assistance, she gathered fir boughs and other plant materials, attached plaid ribbons and pinecones. They decorated the house, barn and cabin, inside and out. Electric candles and colored lights gave everything a warm old-fashioned look.

Ryan said the idea was to make it seem as if they were outdoors, and Susannah felt she'd accomplished that.

Before she could believe it, the night of the dance recital arrived. Nervous to her toes, she nonetheless went out on the floor, determined to enjoy herself.

When she'd dreamed of dancing in a ballet, she'd had much higher aspirations than this, but she couldn't imagine a professional ballerina having more fun than she did that night.

"I wish we got to dance again," Nia said the next morning.

"So do I. But you'll have other recitals."

"I had the prettiest costume. Everybody said so."

"Did they?" The comment made Susannah proud. She'd worked hard to put it together.

"Whatcha doin'?"

"Sending out some invoices for your daddy."

"Huh?"

"Business things. Making sure everybody pays what they owe your daddy for the work he's done."

"Can I play on the computer?"

"No, not right now. I'm using it."

Out of school for the holidays, Nia had nothing to keep her occupied, so she'd come down to the workshop to be with her and Ryan.

She'd been chattering all morning and Susannah was her captive audience. Ryan had left a while ago to finish grouting the last of the tiles for the center dedication.

"Why don't you go outside and play? The sun's shining, and with your gloves and cap on you'll be warm enough."

"I want to stay in here with you."

"Okay, it was just a thought. Why don't you watch a video or play with your dolls?"

"You said you'd help me wrap my present for Daddy."

"I'll help you later. Right now I need to do this."

She put Nia at one of the tables with crayons and paper and told her to draw, but that didn't last. Her attention span today was only fifteen minutes.

"Will you play a game with me?"

"No, honey, I can't. Not right now. I have things I need to get done so your daddy won't have to worry about them after..."

After I'm gone. She couldn't say it out loud, not just because it upset Nia to be reminded that she was going away, but because Susannah's heart ached so badly whenever she thought about it.

The pain would pass; she was certain of it. Once she got to New York amid all the New Year's Eve revelers, she'd be her old self. She'd drop all this useless sentimentality.

And Nia would be fine, too. She probably wouldn't even remember her in a couple of months.

"I wanna wrap Daddy's present."

Susannah blew out a breath and rubbed her temples, where a headache had started to pound. The child was bored. She couldn't fault her for being a little irritating this morning but wished she'd find some way to entertain herself.

"Let me print out the rest of these statements and then I'll stop and help you wrap your gift. But you have to promise to sit there and draw quietly for ten minutes. Can you do it?"

"How long is that?"

Susannah got the timer Ryan sometimes used when he dipped tiles in a chemical bath.

"When the time is up, it makes a noise." She

demonstrated for Nia how it worked, showing her the big hand moving around the dial and counting off one minute.

Nia put her hands over her ears when the buzzer sounded. "That was loud."

"Now I'm going to set it for ten minutes. That's ten times as long as before, so don't get antsy. Think you can be quiet and work on your picture that long?" Nia nodded. "Okay, here we go. No talking or bumping the table or anything until you hear the noise."

Susannah was able to finish the printing before the timer wound down.

"I did it!" Nia yelled.

Susannah took her upstairs and told her to get the gift while she found wrapping paper, tape and scissors.

Nia was excited about the little flannel pouch filled with rocks she planned to give Ryan. She'd collected them a couple of weeks ago during their excursion for fir branches and decorating materials. Ryan sometimes used pebbles and broken china in his mosaics. Nia thought her rocks would be a perfect present.

Susannah had made the pouch out of leftover felt from Nia's costume and a cord drawstring.

"Susannah!" She ran into the den. "I can't find them."

''Look in the drawer of your bedside table. That's where we put them.''

''I did.''

''They have to be there.''

But they weren't. They weren't anywhere. Susannah looked in every conceivable spot in the child's room—the drawers, the closet, under the bed, through her toy chest. She didn't find them in her backpack or under the tree with the rest of the gifts.

''I don't understand it. They didn't grow legs and walk out of here. Did you take them to school or to Gran's?''

''Uh-uh.'' She looked like she was going to cry. ''Now I don't got a present for Daddy.''

''Oh, now, don't worry. We'll find them.''

Susannah searched every crook and cranny in the loft and still came up empty-handed. One day, months from now, the rocks would probably show up in the pocket of a jumper, but for now they weren't anywhere to be found.

''I was bad,'' Nia said, letting out the first pitiful sob. ''The Little People came and got my rocks 'cause I forgot to leave them somethin'.''

''I'm sure that's not it.''

But Nia persisted and couldn't be consoled.

Susannah felt so sorry for her, she was almost in tears herself. She held her. ''Stop crying, okay?

We'll go find some more pretty rocks for your daddy.''

''Now?''

''Yes, now. We'll do it before he gets back. Go wash your face and blow your nose.''

Susannah got their coats. She put a ten in the petty cash box and took out a roll of quarters. These were going to be some expensive rocks.

When they'd bundled up with extra sweaters, scarves, caps, gloves and boots, they set out. Last time, during their excursion into the woods, they'd gone down the driveway. This time they headed the other way, taking a horizontal line from the house.

''There's some over here,'' Nia said. ''I've seen them.'' She picked up a few, but wasn't happy with them. ''I want pretty ones.''

''Those looked nice to me.''

''Over this way.''

''Wait. We can't go too far.''

''I know a good place. Daddy and I go sometimes to get blackberries in the summer.''

They took what appeared to be a trail, climbing for a short spell and then going downhill again.

''How far is it?''

''Up there.''

The terrain got steeper. ''Nia, honey, this doesn't look safe. Take my hand and let's go back. We can find plenty of rocks closer to the house.''

They backtracked, following their footprints until they came to a spot where the trees were so thick the snow covered the ground only in patches. Here there were no footprints to follow.

"This way," Nia said, pulling her to the left.

"Are you sure? I thought we came up by that big oak."

They walked for a few minutes, until Susannah stopped. "This doesn't look right," she said, but she wasn't sure. It *could* be.

"Are you positive this is the way we came?" she asked Nia.

"Mm, maybe it's that way."

Great.

They backtracked again, but she couldn't find the oak. Were they above the house or below it? It was impossible to tell. The hardwood trees were leafless, but the pines and other evergreens formed a canopy. Through them, the only thing Susannah could see was a patch of sky.

A rustling in the bushes startled them both. Whatever was out there was big.

"Nia, honey, come with me. Quietly now. This way."

Hurriedly they went in the other direction. The animal might only have been a deer, but Susannah wasn't taking any chances.

"Are we lost?" Nia asked.

"Oh, no, we're not lost. We simply got turned around. I think I know the way now."

"What about getting my rocks?"

"I see a pretty one over there."

Nia picked it up, decided it would do and asked Susannah to leave one of the quarters.

"Let's see what's over here," Susannah told her once the quarter had been carefully placed on the ground. She decided to head downhill. If they missed the house they'd eventually run into the road. Wouldn't they?

They started, but soon found themselves climbing. The problem was that you had to take a circuitous path to get anywhere. You couldn't go straight up or straight down because of boulders and stands of trees too thick to pass through. Sometimes when it seemed you were going downhill, it turned out only to be the side of a ravine.

Nia selected another rock, and then another. Susannah dutifully left a quarter for each.

After an hour, she stopped so Nia could rest.

She tried to remain calm for the child's sake, but they were in trouble. She checked her watch. After two o'clock. They'd been gone more than three hours. Nia was tired and cold.

Why hadn't she told Annie where they were going? Or called Ryan before they left? Stupid, stupid, stupid! He'd warned her about straying too far from the house. She'd been irresponsible and put both Nia's life and her own in danger.

She tried to figure out what to do. Bass had told her a story the other night about two hikers getting lost in the isolated Snowbird backcountry. They'd used their cell phone to guide the rescue helicopter.

But she didn't have a cell phone. And Ryan had taken his to the center. Those lost hikers had been wise enough to carry supplies. She didn't have matches or even water.

"I'm hungry," Nia said. "And thirsty."

Susannah didn't have anything in her pockets but rocks and a handful of quarters.

"I'm sorry, baby, but we'll be home soon." She took off a glove and scooped up some snow. "Put a little of this in your mouth and let it melt."

If this was summer, she'd stay put and wait. Their chances of surviving until help came would've been good. But night would fall by about four-thirty. And Ryan might not even miss them until much later than that. She had no idea how long he planned to work.

They had to keep moving, to somehow find their way home.

She coaxed Nia into getting up. A sound drew her forward, but she couldn't be certain she was moving toward it or hearing an echo. Rushing water. She saw it now through the trees, a creek and a small waterfall.

She didn't know if it was the same creek she and Ryan had crossed during their hike two weeks ago. Anyway, that information wouldn't help her. She still didn't know which way to go to find the house.

"Can I drink the water?" Nia asked as they approached it.

"No, we'd better not. Sometimes water in the woods has bacteria in it and can make you sick."

"But I'm thirsty," she whined, growing more impatient.

"I know. I am, too. We'll eat more snow."

As before, she knelt, took off her glove and began raking down to a cleaner layer.

"Susannah, I see a pretty gold rock."

"Okay, honey."

If she only had something to scoop with, Nia could crunch the snow as if she were eating it from a cone. She pulled a piece of bark from a nearby tree and found it worked pretty well.

"Try this." Holding the bark piled with snow, she stood and looked up—and lost her breath. Nia had walked out onto rocks in the stream and was bent over the water, reaching for something. "Oh, Nia, no!" She tried to keep panic out of her voice. "Don't move!"

As quickly as she could, Susannah ran toward her.

"But I've almost got it...." Nia said, leaning farther.

"No, don't. You'll—"

Nia's scream as she fell into the water was like a knife in Susannah's heart. She plunged in after her. The shock of the cold was nearly unbearable.

The water was swift. Nia couldn't stand up and was being pulled downstream.

With every ounce of strength Susannah had, she raced after Nia, twice going under before she struggled back to the surface.

Nia grabbed hold of a thin branch hanging over the water and held on, but Susannah knew she couldn't do it for long. Even now, her own limbs and hands were numb with cold.

Finally, she reached her. She crawled onto the bank, dragging Nia behind her by the back of her coat. Violent tremors shook them both. With no shelter and no dry clothes, they had little chance of survival.

"Oh, God!" Susannah cried. "Please let me save this child."

"Sus-ann-ah." Nia tried to say more but had trouble getting it out through her chattering teeth. Susannah realized she was trying to tell her she was sorry.

"Oh, baby, it wasn't your fault," she sobbed. "I'm to blame."

She refused to let this child she loved die. She had to get her bearings and find the house. If only she could see above the trees.

"Lie still and don't move. I'll be right back."

Twice she tried to climb a tree, but her legs didn't want to cooperate. She railed at the heavens, asking for help. On the third attempt, she had better success. The twenty feet she shimmied up the branches didn't allow her to see much, but it was enough.

She'd spotted the sitting dog. And it wasn't too far above them.

SHE CARRIED Nia, forcing her legs to keep moving. The cave, she remembered, was a short walk from the rock. Ryan had matches there and firewood. If she could find it, they'd be all right.

Each step was agonizing. She felt herself drifting off, wanting to stop and rest, but fear, guilt—and love—kept her going.

She found the boards and the brush Ryan had placed over the hidden entrance and threw them aside. She ended up dragging Nia in behind her; the child was too limp to stand.

Nia's trembling had stopped and that scared Susannah. Her body had gone beyond trying to shake off the cold. She had to get the fire started and Nia out of her wet clothes.

The lantern lit easily. She didn't waste time on

the torches, but worked feverishly to get the fire going, every minute that passed feeling like an eternity.

The wood caught fire and began to burn. She stripped Nia of everything and covered her with a blanket she found in Ryan's cache of supplies.

"Come on, baby, stay awake. Nia?" The girl's eyes blinked open. "That's it. Don't go to sleep."

She stripped out of her own clothes and wrapped herself in a second blanket. Kneeling at Nia's legs, she began to rub them briskly with her palms, trying to warm the skin and bring back the circulation.

Every few minutes she'd add more wood to the fire, then rush back and begin rubbing Nia's chilled body again.

Susannah lay down next to her and used what was left of her own body heat to try to warm her.

"Are we gonna die?" Nia whispered, her voice so hoarse she could barely speak.

"No," Susannah told her. "Your ancestors will watch over us."

"SUSANNAH? NIA?"

They weren't in the workshop or upstairs. Ryan went over to the cabin, and although Susannah's truck was there, he didn't get an answer at the door.

He walked back to the barn and dialed the house. His mother hadn't seen them.

"Did they leave a note?" she asked.

"No, I didn't find one. And they've apparently been gone all afternoon because I've called three or four times and left messages. Susannah never returned the calls."

"Maybe they caught a ride over to Helen's."

Unlikely, but he tried anyway. Helen hadn't heard from them.

He called everyone Susannah knew—the ladies from the arts cooperative, John and Bitsy Taylor, Sandy Cummings, Nia's friends. No one had seen either of them.

"Joe." Maybe he'd come by and taken them to town. He caught his brother at his shop.

"Sorry, I haven't seen them since last night."

"I don't like this. Susannah's truck is here. Unless they went off with someone, that leaves only one possibility. And it's nearly dark."

"Get in touch with Bass. I'm on my way."

SUSANNAH WILLED herself not to fall asleep, but it was hard. The drowsiness was like a shroud that kept wanting to wrap her in a warm embrace.

"Must stay awake," she chanted to herself over and over. She stoked the fire again and felt Nia's arms and legs. The color had returned to them and she seemed warmer.

She lit the torches so she could see Ryan's supplies. No food, but she found a small metal boiler and a tin cup.

Nia needed hot liquid. Susannah could use the boiler to melt snow.

She couldn't put on her clothes again until they dried and she couldn't risk getting the blanket wet. She crawled through the opening naked, hastily raked snow into the pan and crawled back inside.

When the liquid was hot, she tested it and poured it in the cup. Propping Nia up, she helped her take tiny sips.

"This will make you feel better. That's right. Drink it all down. Are you feeling warmer?"

"Uh-huh."

Thank God she'd been able to get them here so quickly. Had the cave been another ten minutes away—well, she didn't want to think about that.

She took some of the firewood, stacked it on the other side of the fire and laid their clothes on top to dry. She unbraided Nia's hair so it, too, would dry.

Three more times, Susannah crawled out and got snow to heat. She made Nia drink every drop of the hot liquid.

"How do your toes feel? Wriggle them for me. And your fingers?" They seemed to be working okay.

"I wanna go home."

"I do, too, sweetheart, but we can't yet. We don't

have any warm clothes and it's going to be dark soon.''

That had been the wrong thing to say. The dark scared her. She cried for her daddy, for her grandmother and Nana. Susannah rocked her in her arms.

"We'll be fine. I promise. Daddy will find us.''

Nia's breathing became more erratic, escalating until she began to gasp. She seemed on the verge of a panic attack and Susannah had no way of getting help.

Tears streamed down both their faces. She tried to calm the child by rocking her and talking to her gently.

"Nia, put on my magic ring.'' She slipped it off the chain. "Remember, it gives you courage. Nothing can hurt you as long as you're wearing it.''

She told her stories, about how the redbird got its color, about bat and mouse and why possum had no hair on its tail. Slowly, Nia's breathing eased.

"Do you know that Possum is your daddy's Indian name? Has he ever brought you to this place? Did you know about it?''

Nia shook her head.

Susannah told her the story of her ancestors, about the little boy named Whitepath who had been born in this cave and had lived here with his mother and father.

"His handprint is on the wall over here, along

with your daddy's, his daddy's and even his grand-daddy's. Would you like to see? Keep your blanket wrapped tightly around you.''

Susannah brought the lantern and held it up to the wall. The flames of the fire cast dancing shadows on the pictures.

"See, here's the little boy's. And here's your daddy's.''

"It's too small.''

"That's because he put it here when he was a little boy. One day your handprint will be here, too.''

"No, it won't,'' she said.

"Yes, it will. Every time a child is born in your family they get to put their handprint on the wall. Uncle Joe and Uncle Charlie's are here and Aunt Anita's. You're next.''

She hung her head. "I bet Daddy won't let me,'' she whispered.

"Why on earth would you think that?''

She looked up at Susannah with the most devastated expression she'd ever seen on a child.

"Because I'm not really his little girl.''

CHAPTER THIRTEEN

BASS QUICKLY brought in search parties of deputies, rescue squad members and volunteers, but darkness fell before they could get organized. He wouldn't let anyone go out.

Ryan went ballistic. He ranted and cursed him.

"Dammit, Bass! We can't leave them overnight in this weather! They'll die!"

"I've got a helicopter in the air with spotlights and as soon as they see something, we'll make a rescue, but I'm not sending people out to stumble around in the dark. You know that's not the way. Now, calm down."

"If it was your wife and daughter out there—"

"I wouldn't do a damn thing differently and you know it."

Joe pulled him back. "Ryan, come on. He'll move heaven and earth to find them."

Ryan felt shamed by his actions. Bascombe Miller had been his best friend all his life. He loved Nia like his own.

He nearly broke down. "I'm sorry, Bass. I just feel so useless. If anything happens to them…"

Bass put one hand on his shoulder. "The best thing you can do right now is help me do my job. You know this mountain better than anyone. When the helo spots them, we have to be ready to move. We need you to lead us. Stay strong."

Ryan steeled his courage and nodded.

"We'll find them," Joe said. "Now help me calm Mom and Nana. They're insane with worry."

"NIA, I don't understand what you're saying."

"I'm not his little girl."

Susannah knelt and took her by the arms. "Honey, what makes you think that?"

"I heard Mommy tell the man in the black dress. He came to help her go to heaven."

A man in a…? The priest. Carla had wanted to die at home in her own bed, according to Ryan. She must have asked for the priest to hear her confession.

"I wasn't supposed to be in there," Nia said, "but I forgot Cooper. I sneaked in her room to get him."

"What did you hear your mother tell the man in the black dress?"

"She said Daddy wasn't my real daddy, but he'd be good to me."

Oh, Lord! For months this poor child had gone through the anguish of believing she didn't belong to the one person she cared for the most.

Could she be right? And if so, did Ryan know?

"Don't tell him I'm not *Tsalagi*," Nia pleaded.

Now Susannah understood fully. Nia reasoned that if she wasn't Ryan's child, she wasn't Cherokee. And if he found that out, he might not want her.

How tragic that Ryan's strong pride in his heritage had caused such pain for his daughter.

"Nia, come over here and sit down. I want to talk to you." They crossed back to the fire. "Cover up. That's good. Not too long ago, your daddy told me a story. He said the first time he saw you he thought you were the most special thing on earth. He knew he'd love you forever and ever."

"Like Uncle Bass loves Maggie?"

"Exactly like that."

"But she's his real little girl. He has to."

"Well, daddies do love their real little girls. That's true. But they can also love little girls who aren't theirs. Uncle Bass and Aunt Helen are going to adopt a child. Do you know what adopt means?"

"A little boy or girl don't got a mommy or daddy?"

"Mm, that's close enough. Bass and Helen will be the mommy and daddy. And they'll love that child just as much as Maggie. You don't have to be people's real little girl for them to love you.''

''Daddy loves me.''

''Yes, he does and he will, no matter what. You see, love doesn't depend on whether you're born to someone or not, or even if you're *Tsalagi* or white. Love is just the way you feel.''

Sometimes, Susannah realized, it could even happen when it was the last thing you were looking for.

''Now, let's lie down and try to rest.'' She covered Nia and lay with one arm around her.

''Susannah?''

''Yes, baby?''

''I love *you*.''

She stroked Nia's head and shed silent tears. ''I love you, too.''

THROUGHOUT THE NIGHT, more and more people arrived as word spread, neighbors wanting to join the search party, women bringing hot coffee and food for the searchers.

Using the house as the center, the helicopter made an ever widening circle, but hour after hour passed with no news. Expressions turned grim. Ryan started hearing words like *hopeless* and *impossible*.

Helen had come over with the baby and was holding vigil with his mother and grandmother at the house. He was thankful for that. He couldn't deal with them right now, couldn't pretend everything was going to be okay.

He thought about calling Anita, but she was supposed to be home tomorrow anyway. No use getting her up in the middle of the night.

Charlie, Barbara and the kids were scheduled to arrive the day after and stay through Christmas. If the news was bad, he'd call them tomorrow.

But he couldn't think about that now. He couldn't allow his faith to waver. Like Bass said, he had to stay strong.

A MOURNFUL HOWL startled Susannah in the night. She wondered if she'd dreamed it. Or perhaps the sitting dog was calling for her mate.

Again she heard it. Low, sorrowful.

She put more wood on the fire and checked to make sure the barrier she'd erected over the entry was secure. The dark she could handle, but wild animals were something else.

Nia had finally fallen asleep. Susannah hoped she'd stay that way until morning.

She had no idea of the time. Her watch had gotten water in it and stopped. But their clothes had dried, with the exception of their coats, and being able to dress again had made them both feel safer, somehow.

The cave was warm. The ground was hard, difficult to sleep on, but she could stand it. Before dark, she'd gathered enough snow and melted drinking water in case they needed it during the night.

Nothing would stop the growl of hunger in her belly, but help would surely come in the morning. It *had* to come. The wood was running out. They didn't have enough for another night.

She could chance finding her way down the mountain tomorrow. Or she might have to risk their remaining wood on an outside fire where searchers would be more likely to see the smoke.

How many days, she wondered, could they survive here without food?

She lay down, exhausted and afraid, at Nia's back and pulled the blanket over the child's shoulders. The smoke curled upward and out the hole in the rock above and she watched its lazy journey until her lids began to get heavy.

Ryan had told her once that fire was a messenger and that smoke carried your prayers where they were supposed to go.

She wanted to believe it. Right now she *needed* to believe it.

"If you're listening up there," she whispered, "this is Susannah. And I have a favor to ask...."

DAWN BROKE. Search teams of men from Sitting Dog and Robbinsville started a grid-by-grid search of the mountain. John Taylor from the store, accompanied by ten men, headed east. Joe and his group took the area from the house down to the road. Bass and his party headed for the slope to the west.

Ryan felt it unlikely Susannah and Nia had gone up the mountain, but he couldn't be sure. He knew the top reaches better than anyone, so he led a group of five men and made a quick sweep above the house.

Bass told them that if they didn't find signs they should break up and join the searchers to the east and west.

They were twenty minutes out when one of the sheriff's deputies called to him from his right.

"Mr. Whitepath?"

"Yeah?"

"What do you make of this?"

Ryan rushed over. The man handed him a quarter. "I found it here by this rock. And look, there's another one. And a third."

"Paying the Little People," Ryan muttered.

"Who?"

"My daughter," he said, getting excited. "She's been here."

"SUSANNAH!" The voice called from far away.

"I'm coming, Mama."

She sat up, rubbing the sleep from her eyes and fighting the fog that clouded her mind.

For a moment she thought she was home, back in her old room and the call of her name had come from the adjoining bedroom.

"Susannah!"

There it was again. This time she shot up straight.

The woods. The water. The cave. She realized where she was.

"Susannah!"

That voice! That gloriously wonderful voice.

"Ryan! Ryan, in here!" Hurriedly, she put on her boots and began clawing at the timbers blocking the passage. "We're in here!"

"Susannah?"

"Yes, yes, we're here. Oh, Ryan!"

He was working as frantically from the other side as she was from hers. Nia woke. She began echoing Susannah's cries, calling out for her daddy.

Ryan pushed through the barrier and took Susannah into his arms. Nia ran to him and he bent and scooped her up.

"Are you all right? Are you hurt?"

Susannah was so overwhelmed she burst into tears. Words came pouring out. "We were looking for rocks and we got lost, and I thought we were going the right way, but we weren't and there was a bear or something so we ran away and then Nia fell into the water and got wet and I didn't know what else to do and I remembered the sitting dog and thank God I found the cave or we would have died and—''

"Hush, you're safe now. You're both safe."

"Ryan?" Bass called from outside. "I've got a paramedic team here."

Ryan crawled out first and led Nia. Susannah followed. Someone threw a shiny blanket around her shoulders and began taking her pulse and asking her questions.

"I'm okay. Take care of Nia."

"She's in good hands. Don't worry."

Looking past the man's shoulder, she saw the child held in the safety of her father's arms.

"Yes, you're right about that."

ASIDE FROM a few cuts and bruises, Susannah was fine.

Nia didn't seem to have suffered any ill effects from her night on the mountain, but the hospital in Andrews wanted to keep her a few hours for observation and to bring her body temperature up a few degrees, back to normal.

She was still in the emergency room, having an X ray made of her chest.

"Let me have Joe drive you home," Ryan told

Susannah as they waited in the hall. "You look beat."

"I want to stay."

He took her hand and held on tightly. "Okay."

"Did you call your mother? She'll be worried."

"When I got your coffee and sandwich."

She thought about her harrowing experience and wanted to cry all over again. But mostly, she wanted to cry for Ryan, for the thing she had to tell him.

"People know about your cave now," she said. "Will that be a problem?"

"I don't think so. Except for Bass, they thought it was a bear cave. And not even he's been inside."

"Why not? I thought that as boys the two of you probably spent a lot of time there."

"No, only me. The cave is for our family."

"But you took *me* there."

"And why do you think I did that?"

"I don't know. Until this moment, I didn't realize I was so privileged."

"Maybe you should give it some thought."

"I will, but right now I have something…I need to tell you some things. They're important."

"I'm listening."

"First, I'm sorry. My irresponsibility nearly got Nia killed. I should never have taken her into the woods."

"Beating yourself up over it now won't help."

"I don't understand why you aren't angry."

"I guess I should be, but I'm so relieved you're both okay that being angry seems counterproductive. Besides, Nia told me what you did for her, how she fell in the water and you jumped in after her. I know you don't swim well."

"That never crossed my mind. All I could think of was that she'd drown if I didn't get to her."

"I know how well you took care of her at the cave, too. She said you heated water for her and kept her warm. The walking around naked part tickled her a bit. I'd like to have seen that myself."

Across the corridor on the other bench, Joe overheard and laughed.

"Could you find a nurse to flirt with while your brother and I have a private chat?" Susannah asked him.

"Yeah, I can do that." He got up and started to walk away.

"Hey, Joe," she called after him. He turned. "Ryan said you stayed with him all night and led a search party to look for us this morning. Thank you."

"No problem. Glad you're okay." He ambled off.

"What was I saying? Oh, at the time, being naked wasn't very funny. I heard the sitting dog, I think. I heard *something* howl. I thought it might try to come into the cave."

"A red wolf maybe. Once they were nearly hunted to extinction, but they've been reintroduced into the mountains in recent years. It's unusual to hear one, though."

"The whole night was unusual. I asked the fire to send my prayers to the sky."

"And it was the smoke that led me to you."

"You saw it?"

"No, the haze obscured it, but I smelled it on the wind. I knew that if you had fire you could only be in one place."

She couldn't believe it.

"I hoped you'd think to look for us there."

He told her about finding her quarters and knowing he was heading in the right direction. "But I was afraid you might be hurt. The woods are full of wild Russian boar and they can be aggressive."

"Physically, I was fine, but emotionally I wasn't doing too well. I never want to go through another night like that."

"Nia said you told her stories about the animals to keep her from being afraid. You've learned well, *To tsu hwa*. You make a good Cherokee."

"A redheaded, white-skinned, freckle-faced, blue-eyed Cherokee. Now, that's one for the record books."

"What makes you Cherokee isn't here." He rubbed his fingers across the pale skin of her palm.

"What makes you Cherokee is in here." He placed her palm against her heart.

"Is that really true?"

"Yes. It's not the blood that makes you *Tsalagi* but the practice of the ways of our tribe."

"Your daughter needs to understand that."

"She does understand."

"No, she doesn't. Let's step outside where we won't be overheard. There's something you should know, and it may be the hardest thing you ever have to hear."

RYAN SANK DOWN on the concrete wall as Susannah delivered her news, his legs unable to support him.

"Do you know for certain she's your biological daughter?" Susannah asked.

"She's not."

She, too, sat down. "I wasn't sure if it was true, and whether or not you knew. I've been in agony all night, wondering how I was going to break the news to you."

"I've known almost from the beginning. But it never mattered. In every way that counts, she's my child."

"Does your family know?"

"No, well…" He hesitated. "Not Mom or my brothers and sister. Nana I'm not sure about. I've never come out and told her, but she has an uncanny way of knowing things."

"I'm catching on to that."

"My arrangement with Carla was that I'd raise Nia as my own, but she could never tell anyone the truth. I felt it was better not to mention it to my own family, in case they let something slip to Nia."

"The father? Who is he?"

"He was her lover before me, an English businessman she met through her job at the gallery. He already had a wife and three children. When she called him and said she was pregnant, that the child might be his, he told her to get rid of it and not bother him again. But she was Catholic. And she couldn't be sure which of us was the father until Nia was born."

"You had blood tests after her birth?"

"Yes, but by then I no longer cared about the results. Carla said she'd put the baby up for adoption, but I couldn't let her. I'd been abandoned in a way by my own father. I wasn't a child at the time, but I remembered the hurt of knowing he didn't want to be with us."

"I know that pain is still with you."

"That little baby deserved better. I had Carla list me as the father on the birth certificate and I agreed to raise her."

"Nia's hurting. She's been afraid you'd find out

she's not your blood child, not *Tsalagi,* and
wouldn't want her.''

"Had I known this was causing her problems…
Not once in all these months did it occur to me that
she might have learned the truth.''

"She never would have if she hadn't overheard
Carla's confession.''

"What should I do?''

"I don't know. You should talk to Dr. Thompson
about this.''

"I will, but Nia opened up to you, not the therapist. In fact, her doctor was so far off base, I'm not
sure I trust her advice.''

"That's unfair. Dr. Thompson's done the best she
could with the information she had. If *you* didn't
suspect what the problem was with Nia, how can
you blame the therapist?''

"I guess I want someone to blame other than
myself.''

"I don't see a reason to blame anyone. Be thankful you finally know what's been hurting her.''

"Which brings me back to the question of what
I should do.''

"Ryan, I…all right. If I were Nia…I'd want to
know that *you* know the truth and have always loved
me anyway.''

"So, you're saying I should be honest with her.''

"I would, about that part. The rest, I'm not at all

sure what to tell you. She'll probably ask where her real father is and you need to be prepared to answer that. But should you tell her the truth now? If you do, could she be hurt at knowing *he* didn't want her? She might. But she might also be relieved to know he'll never come to take her away from you."

"What do you think?"

"The latter. That she'll be relieved. But I can't be certain of that."

"This is so damn confusing. I don't really know how to handle it."

"Just remember, whatever you do, that she won't always be six. Sooner or later she'll be old enough to ask questions and get information from sources other than you."

"Meaning if I lie to her now, she could find out twenty years from now and hate me for it."

"Possibly. I'm wondering if there's a way to be both honest with her about her biological father, yet give her the reassurance she needs. Try to reach her doctor before you talk to her."

"I will."

"Oh!" She sucked in a breath.

"What?"

"I have an idea. I think I know a way to help her accept that she's truly part of your family."

CHAPTER FOURTEEN

HAD ANYONE TOLD Ryan he'd be taking Nia back up the mountain two days later, he wouldn't have believed it.

"Here, Sa Sa. Ride on my back a while and rest your legs."

She put her arms around his neck and he picked her up.

"Why didn't Susannah come?" she asked as they continued to climb.

"Because what we're about to do is special. She felt we needed to be alone."

"I don't have to spend the night, do I?"

"No, don't worry. We'll only stay a few minutes. We'll be back in time to begin our celebration of the Winter Solstice."

"We'll light the big fire and the tree outside."

"Yes, and as dawn comes, we'll welcome the return of the sun. That's why we celebrate. Do you understand?"

"Mmm. It's Christmas?"

"Nearly. We honor the rhythms of the earth and

the sun because they make our seasons—winter when everything's cold and the animals rest; spring when the seeds begin to push their heads up through Nana's garden; summer when there's plenty of light and the animals are at play; and fall when the earth gets sleepy and the animals store their food.''

"I like summer 'cause we get to eat Nana's tomatoes.''

"Me, too,'' he said with a chuckle. "Do you know what season this is?''

"Winter.''

"Right. And today is what we call *midwinter,* the shortest day of the year. Night will come early. Little by little, ever since summer, the days have been getting shorter. But after tonight the days will begin to get longer again.''

"And that's good 'cause we can play outside.''

"Absolutely. That's the best reason of all.''

They reached the cave. Nia was a bit reluctant to go inside until he reminded her of what they were here to do.

He went first and helped her through the opening.

"I should've brought you here before,'' he said, lighting the torches so they could see.

Ryan had told his family the truth. And he'd told Nia. Her biological father, like her mother, hadn't been in a position to keep her, he'd explained, but Ryan had wanted her very much as *his* little girl.

His words had been enough for her—for now. Later, as she grew older and could understand adult relationships better, he'd answer whatever questions she asked.

He took the tin of paint and mixed some with water in the wooden bowl. He helped her dip her hand in the paint and press it against the wall next to his own.

"Spirits of my ancestors, see this little one and know she belongs to me and to our family. *Aquetsi.*" *My child.*

With the small brush he'd brought, they printed her Indian name under her handprint.

"I'm a Whitepath now, Daddy?"

"Yes, Sa Sa, you're a Whitepath."

SUSANNAH FELT the bedsprings dip and the warm body slide in next to her under the covers.

"Nap time's over," Ryan whispered in her ear, nipping at her earlobe. He reached under her T-shirt and rubbed her back, then slipped his hand down into her panties. "Time to get up."

"Leave me alone. I'm tired."

"You've slept half the day."

"Because you kept me up all night."

"I thought you liked our celebration."

"I loved it, but you wouldn't let me go to bed

until we greeted the sun. A girl's got to get her beauty rest.''

''You're beautiful enough.''

''Ha! What time is it?''

''One.''

''Uh. Too early. Go away. Come back in a couple of hours.''

''You can't lounge around in bed all day.''

''I can try. Where's Nia?''

''At my mom's eating lunch with the family.''

''Everyone's up already?''

''Everyone but you. They sent me to get you.''

''Agh!''

She'd truly enjoyed last night's Solstice rituals, but she didn't operate well on five hours' sleep.

He reached around and stroked her breasts. ''Not fair,'' she mumbled. His hand moved between her legs. Against her will they opened for him, letting him dip into her moisture. ''Really, really not fair.''

She rolled over onto her back and let him touch wherever he wanted with his hands and mouth, until she was so aroused she couldn't get him out of his clothes fast enough.

''Did they tell you to wake me up this way?'' she asked breathlessly.

He slipped on a condom, hooked her legs around him and slid into her. ''No, this was my own idea.''

Moving together furiously, too impatient for finesse, they rocked the old bed until it sounded like a rocket ship about to blast into orbit.

"I need to oil this thing."

"You or the bed?" she joked.

"Hell, not me!"

She raked her nails along his back, exciting him more, as she knew it would. They were both nearly at the edge.

"This is better than an alarm clock anyday," she said.

"I'm glad you think so. I'll wake you up like this every morning from now on."

She stilled beneath him, but she was so close to her orgasm that it surged through her anyway, sending her arching off the bed. With a roar he climaxed a moment later.

She'd never felt so physically wonderful and so emotionally miserable at the same instant.

He collapsed on top of her. She was afraid to move, afraid to speak.

"What happened there at the end?" he asked when he'd recovered. "Why did you stop?"

"Let me up so I can go to the bathroom." She kept her head turned away, but he made her look at him.

"Is something wrong? Hey, are you crying?"

"Ryan, let me up, please."

"No, tell me what's wrong."

"Ryan, please let me up!"

He did.

She ran to the bathroom and stayed a long time. Hiding was more like it. Being a coward. While she was in the shower, she heard him come in and clean up at the sink, but he said nothing.

Wrapped in a towel, she finally emerged. Ryan sat on the couch with his back to her, already dressed. She quickly pulled on her clothes.

"You're still planning to leave the day after tomorrow, aren't you?" he said, without turning.

She couldn't speak. Her voice wouldn't come out of her throat. But she didn't need to give an answer. He already knew.

He got up and faced her, his expression stony. "I thought…I hoped you'd changed your mind."

"No, I haven't."

He grabbed his jacket and stalked toward the door.

"Ryan, wait! Don't be angry. We have to talk about this."

"Talk? Hell, Susannah! You already know how I feel about you. I've asked you to stay with me. What else do you want me to say? That I'm in love with you? I am. That I want to marry you and spend our lives together raising our daughter? I do. But if you don't love me, I can't force you to. Things are as simple as that."

As he went out, he slammed the door. Susannah sank down on her knees and wept.

RYAN AVOIDED HER the rest of the day. If she went to the workshop, he went to the house. If she went to the house, he found something to do in the workshop.

The tension between them was so obvious that even Nia noticed it.

"Are you and Daddy mad?" she asked.

Everyone in the room stopped talking and turned to look at her.

"No, honey, not really. He's a bit sad because I'm leaving. Remember I told you it's nearly time for me to go away? We talked about this. You promised me you'd be really brave."

"Nana Sipsey says you won't go. You're the redbird with the broken wing. The spirits sent you to help me."

Susannah cocked her head questioningly at Nana. The old woman nodded.

"You're wrong this time," she told her.

"Hmph," she said, her expression smug.

"You aren't really going away, are you, Susannah?" Nia asked.

"Yes, sweetheart, I am."

Nia's little face fell. She pulled off the ring Susannah had let her wear the night in the cave. "I better give this back. You might need the magic."

"No, I want you to keep it. My mother gave it to me with love. I gave it to you the same way."

"Will you ever come back?"

She wanted to say she would, but she refused to make a promise she couldn't keep.

"I hope so, Nia. But if I don't, you have my name on Cooper and my ring. And I saved my cast with your name on it. I'll never throw it away."

"Promise?"

"I promise."

LATER THAT EVENING she decided she couldn't bear staying here two more days. Dragging out her good-byes when it was painful for everyone was stupid. Better to make a quick, clean break and get a head start on her holiday plans than spend the next forty-eight hours in misery. She'd leave in the morning.

Willing herself not to cry, she pulled out her suitcase and began packing. This was the right thing to do, wasn't it? Her grief was still too new and her feelings too tender to make a permanent commitment, and remaining would only confuse Nia and prevent Ryan from finding someone else to share his life.

Someone else.

"Don't think about it," she warned herself. She couldn't afford tears right now, and focusing on who might come along to take her place in Ryan's heart would only produce them.

Wrapping her remaining Christmas gifts for the family, she loaded them in the truck and drove back to the house. For Nia she had a new jumper and blouse. For Nana a lovely hat for church.

She'd blown up some of the photographs she'd taken at Thanksgiving and had them matted. Annie was going to love the family portrait. Charlie had his own shot with Barbara and the kids. Anita's photo was a pose of her with her mother and grandmother.

Joe had been a problem. Borrowing Annie's sewing machine, she'd made him a quilted jacket, sleeveless like he preferred to wear. And Ryan. His gift had stumped her. Nothing she could imagine making him was good enough, so she'd cheated. She'd wrapped an eight-by-ten photograph of him and Nia that she'd taken, but also bought him an expensive set of grinding tools he'd admired in a catalog.

Joe came out and helped her get everything into the house and under the tree. Ryan had emerged from his workshop several hours ago, but then taken off in the truck.

"I'll be leaving in the morning," she announced. "I want to tell you all while I have the chance that I appreciate your hospitality. Thank you for letting me be a part of your family for these last two months.''

"Susannah, please don't,'' Annie appealed to her. "Wait until Christmas. You'll miss the dedication of Ryan's mosaic tomorrow night and you've worked so hard on that. And Christmas—you have to stay and open presents with us.''

"I think it's best if I go. I have a long way to drive over the next week and it'll be easier if I get an early start.''

"Does Ryan know?''

"No, I haven't spoken with him,'' she said, trying not to cry. "I'll be leaving very early, so I won't see you again.'' She kissed them all.

"You've become like my own daughter,'' Ryan's mother told her. "Remember you always have a home with us.''

"Thank you, Annie. That means a great deal to me.''

Annie suggested they open presents that night so Susannah could enjoy hers. Susannah said they shouldn't; she told them to go ahead with their normal plans.

"At least take the ones we made you,'' Annie said. "Save them for Christmas morning and think of us.''

"I will.'' Joe brought them down to the cabin for her.

A while later, while she was packing, Ryan knocked softly. "Susannah?"

Her face was tearstained, but she no longer cared. She opened the door and they stared at each other.

"Hi," he said.

"Hi. Um, would you like to come in?"

"No, I'd better not. I see you're packing."

"I was going to come over and talk to you, but I didn't know you were home yet."

"Mother called me on my cell phone and said you'd decided to leave in the morning."

"Yes, I think it's best for both of us if I do."

"You don't have to, Susannah. I know I've been a bastard today, but being near you..."

"That's okay, Ryan. Being near you has been hard for me, too."

"You don't have to go. Stay for the dedication. Don't you want to see the mural?"

"I'm sure it's beautiful. You're the most talented man I've ever met."

"Please stay."

"I can't. It would be too hard."

He nodded slowly. "I understand."

"How does Nia feel about my leaving?"

"She's upset, but don't worry. She'll be fine."

"I hope this won't cause a setback in her progress."

"No, the doctor says she has some distance to go

before she gets well, but she's made a strong start. The two of them have talked a couple of times by phone and Nia's finally willing to discuss her mother. This morning I noticed she'd taken her mother's photographs out and put them in her room.''

"That's good, Ryan. I'm happy for her and for you.''

"She wanted to be sure I brought these over.'' He handed her a shopping bag. "Gifts from the two of us.''

"Thank you. I left yours at the house.'' She remembered something. "Oh, just a minute.'' She ran inside and came back with a package of photographs. "I'd be grateful if you'd give this to Helen and Bass for me. Tell them…tell them I wish them all the happiness in the world and that I hope the adoption comes through soon.''

"I will.''

"Strange, isn't it, this world we live in? Nia wanted to be Cherokee because she thought that was the only way she'd be accepted by her Cherokee father. And little Maggie will probably one day wish she was white so her white grandparents will accept *her*.''

"Not strange. Sad that we can't see past the color of each other's skin.'' He stared at her again for a minute in silence. "Well," he said finally. "I'd better go."

"Thank you, Ryan. For everything. For what you've taught me. For...being you." She began to cry and couldn't go on.

He leaned in and kissed her. They clung to each other for a moment. "Be happy, Susannah. I hope you find what you're looking for."

And then he turned and was gone.

THE DINER next to the motel was nearly deserted. A couple occupied the booth next to the front window and a truck driver was working on his third cup of black coffee at the counter two seats over.

The man and woman were headed north to Virginia to spend Christmas with their son, Susannah had heard them tell the waitress. The driver was hauling pipe the other way, south to Florida.

"Anything else?" the waitress asked her.

"No, thank you." She opened her wallet and handed her a ten.

"Ah, what a cute little girl. Yours?"

"No, a friend's."

"What's her name?"

"Sa Sa." She touched the photo and felt an overwhelming longing.

"Strange name for a kid."

"It's a nickname. In Cherokee it means goose or swan."

"She's a real doll."

"Yes, she is."

She gave Susannah her change. "Merry Christmas. Hope you have a good one with your family."

"Yes, I will. Same to you."

Back in her room, there was nothing on TV worth watching and she didn't have a book. The motel had a selection of movies, any of which you could rent and have delivered to the room, but nothing appealed to her.

Where, she wondered, was the enthusiasm she'd expected to feel?

She was on the road again and should be bursting with excitement at what lay ahead. Instead, her thoughts turned not to what was in front of her but what she'd left behind, a man and a child she'd come to love.

The clock by the bed said eight. The dedication would be over by now. The Whitepaths were probably gathered around the kitchen table eating supper.

Nana would be fussing about people not eating enough. Nia and her cousins would be getting anxious about Santa's visit in a few hours.

And Ryan. What would he be doing? Thinking of her the way she was thinking of him?

She went out to the truck and got the shopping

bag containing his and Nia's presents and the other gifts from the family. She'd be traveling tomorrow. The thought of waking up in a motel room on Christmas morning and opening presents by herself was pretty depressing. She'd have her own little Christmas party tonight and avoid the morning blues, thank you very much.

She laid everything on the bed and opened the packages one by one. Ryan's mother had woven a beautiful basket for her. Nana had embroidered a hand towel.

Anita had fashioned her earrings from beautiful shells. Joe had carved a deer out of wood.

Even Charlie, whom she'd hardly gotten to know, had made her something. He'd built and painted her a whimsical whirligig in the shape of a duck.

If she only had a yard, she'd have a place to put it.

She opened Nia's present next. The drawing was of a house with a mommy, daddy and little girl. "I love you," she'd printed across the top.

Susannah wiped her eyes.

Ryan had put two presents in the sack, a rectangular box and an envelope. "Open me first," a note on the box said.

Inside was a videotape. She put it into the VCR on the top of the TV and pushed the "play" button on the remote.

Opening credits began to roll. *Christmas on Snowbird Mountain,* they read. *Starring Susannah Pelton.*

She let out a squeal. How had he done this?

She watched the movie with delight. It was hilarious and included a commentary by someone whose voice she didn't recognize.

There she was singing while they worked on the mural. And they'd taken video of her performing in the recital!

All those times Joe and Ryan had pulled out the camera and she hadn't suspected this was what they were doing. The "movie" showed her climbing the mountain that day on the way to the hot springs. And, oh God, here she was with Nia, reading a bedtime story, playing Chutes and Ladders and making their decorations!

How precious this was. "Oh, Ryan."

She opened the envelope. Inside was a note in his handwriting that said:

Susannah,

I hope you enjoyed being the star of your own movie. You can mark that one off your list. I didn't know how to go about getting you on a cruise down the Amazon, but if you'll call the number below, a round-trip airline ticket has been reserved in your name to use whenever you want. I understand Paris is beautiful in April.

Love forever,
Ryan

CHAPTER FIFTEEN

RYAN TRIED to stay upbeat and not put a damper on everyone's Christmas morning, but it was tough when he was hurting so much inside.

The children, at least, were having fun. They squealed as they played with their toys and ran through the house. Wrapping paper lay discarded everywhere.

He'd given Nia the stroller she wanted and the doll she'd been begging for that went with it, the baby that wet and cried. Now, he could see, he'd live to regret it. She'd forced him to bottle feed and diaper the thing ten times already.

"The baby's hungry, Daddy," she said again.

"The baby's going to get sick if you keep making me feed it."

"Uh-uh, she tee tees it out."

"So I noticed." The diapers weren't completely waterproof. He had a big wet spot on his shirt.

She pushed its stomach and it cried again to be fed.

Nana Sipsey, sitting next to him on the couch,

patted his leg and told him she'd take over nursery duty. He might want to go out on the porch and get some air.

"Thanks. I could use it."

He handed over all the doll paraphernalia. Grabbing his jacket, he went out and sat on the top step. A few minutes later, Joe joined him.

"Too much noise for me," his brother told him. "I don't see how Charlie and Barb stand it. That little one is a real terror. How come if he can't talk he can scream so loud?"

"Wait until you have four of five of your own running around. You'll think their voices are music."

"No way. Kids are too loud and too sticky."

"They don't always smell good, either, but I promise it won't matter when you get ready to settle down."

"I'll never be ready for that. Give me wine, women and more women."

"You're hopeless. You know that?"

"Yeah, but having a hell of a good time."

They both looked off down the drive at the sound of a vehicle. Ryan stood as a familiar gray truck came closer. He wanted to fly from the porch and meet it, but pride wouldn't let him.

"Well, I'll be," Joe said, getting up. "Look who decided to come back. Wonder why?" He grinned and slapped Ryan on the back. "I think I'll go in and let you two have a private reunion."

So many cars and trucks were in the yard, she had to park down the driveway a bit. She got out, walked to the house and stopped at the bottom of the steps.

His heart felt like a lead weight inside his chest. What was she doing here? He was afraid to be happy, afraid she'd simply forgotten something or wanted to tell him off in person for his plane ticket gift.

"I thought you'd be halfway to New York City by now," he said.

"So did I."

"Why aren't you?"

"Because I finally realized what an idiot I am. I've been searching for something that's been in front of me all this time."

He didn't dare breathe. "And what's that?"

"Real life."

"Real life isn't very exciting."

"Isn't it? Oh, I don't know." She walked up the steps and faced him. "I can't think of anything that will give me more of an adrenaline rush than playing the tooth fairy, taking my little girl to ballet lessons or winding down at the end of the day by talking to the man I love."

"Susannah, be sure."

"I am sure. I love you, Ryan. I love Nia. I love

your mother and Nana and Joe. I'm certain I'll come to love Anita and Charlie when I know them better.''

"And what happens in three months or six months when you get the itch to go ramble or jump off a bridge?''

"Why would I want to go anywhere when the best place on earth is this mountain? I've created something beautiful, had sex with a handsome stranger and starred in my very own movie. That should be enough to satisfy any person for a lifetime. Oh, and I've danced in a ballet. You had something to do with that last one, too, didn't you?''

"I might have.''

"I suspected it when I watched the movie, which I loved by the way. The movie was on my list and so was the ballet. I figured if you had a hand in the first, you probably did with the second.''

"I got Joe to ask Sandy to find you a part in the recital. I wanted you to be happy. And if dancing and being in a movie got you a step closer to that goal, then I felt I had to try and give them to you.''

"You were wrong. I was wrong, too. I don't need anything to be happy but you…and Nia.''

"What about Paris?''

"When I held your note in my hand and realized I could fulfill that dream, I didn't want it. I really don't care about the Eiffel Tower. I have Snowbird.

Eating French onion soup in a sidewalk café can't compare to cheese and bread on a rock that looks like a sitting dog.''

He reached out and touched her face. ''I love you so much. When you left, I died inside a little bit.''

''I'm sorry I hurt you. I believed I was past my grief, but I wasn't. I ran from what we have because it hurt to care for someone and to have someone care for me. But I'll never run again. I promise you.'' She stepped closer and put her arms around his waist. ''Will you forgive me for being such a fool?''

''Every day for the rest of my life.''

He kissed her and a cheer went up from inside the house. They laughed at the faces in the windows, everyone pressed to the glass watching them.

''We have an audience,'' he said. ''And I warn you, they can be a rowdy bunch.''

''Then let's really give them something to hoot about.''

''My pleasure.''

''NANA WAS RIGHT!'' Nia shouted, throwing herself into Susannah's arms. ''You're here! You're here.''

Susannah laughed and twirled her around. ''I missed you, too.''

''Nana said if I wrote what I wanted on my leaf for the tree, it would come true. See?''

She took her by the hand and pulled her over to the little wishing tree. Susannah looked at the leaf with Nia's name on the front. Someone had helped her print her wish in Cherokee. "What does it say?"

"That I wish you'd come and live with me and Daddy."

She glanced up at Ryan and he winked. "Sounds like a great idea to me," he told his daughter. "But maybe we should marry her first."

"Really? We're gonna get married? All three of us?"

"All three of us," Susannah assured her. "I can't walk down the aisle without you."

"Yippee!" Nia started jumping up and down. "We're getting married!" she told her grandmother.

Susannah was hugged and kissed and crushed all over again by every person in the room.

"Can you handle all this attention?" Ryan asked. "This family tends to be a bit demonstrative."

"Are you kidding? I love it! I never thought I'd ever be part of a family again."

"Come with me." He pulled her away and out the front door. "I want you all to myself."

"Do you still have the key to the center? Take me there and show me your mosaic."

"Right now? I had something else in mind."

"Please?"

"Whatever you want."

He drove them over and unlocked the front door. When they got to the extension, he told her to close her eyes. She heard him flip on the lights. He guided her inside and around the tables and chairs that had been set up for last night's dedication of the room and the mural.

"Okay, ready? Open your eyes."

She stood and stared, taking it all in. She'd seen most of it, of course, but the effect of the whole piece was glorious. And the vignette of the White-paths on the last panel...

"Oh, Ryan!"

He had them around the kitchen table in a scene that was so familiar. Nana sat peeling potatoes into a pan. His mother and siblings had gathered around like they often did when they helped prepare a meal.

The scene represented home and family.

And she was there with them, standing next to Ryan. They both had their hands on Nia's shoulders. He'd even managed to work in her snowbirds by showing part of the outdoors through the kitchen window.

She walked over and touched the tiles, the faces of her soon-to-be family. The nearby plaque said the mosaic had been designed and created by Ryan Whitepath...with help from Susannah Pelton.

"It's wonderful. But you shouldn't have given me any credit."

"I couldn't have done it without you. We created something beautiful, and like you said, people will appreciate it for years to come."

"But why did you include me with your family? You couldn't have known I'd come back."

"You were part of us from the very beginning, even if you didn't realize it. Our own little redbird with a broken wing who came to our mountain one day and changed all our lives."

"Nana Sipsey and her vision."

"She told you?"

"Nia did. But I didn't understand all of it."

"Nana said you'd heal Nia of her grief and pain. And that you'd heal yourself…"

"She was right. I do feel as if I've finally put the past behind me. I loved my mother, and I miss her more than I can ever express, but it's time to move beyond her illness and what it did to both our lives. She wouldn't want me to continue to suffer."

"No, she wouldn't."

"And Andrew…God! He *was* a jerk. I can't imagine why I've been stupid enough to grieve over what he did. I'm glad he left me. Otherwise, I never would've met you. I finally understood last night, how lucky I am to get a second chance at happiness. I wondered what on earth I was doing, sitting alone in a motel room on Christmas Eve when I could be with the man and the child I love. Nothing can compare with Christmas on this mountain.''

''Not even April in Paris?''

''Especially not that.''

''I'll take you to Paris on our honeymoon, if you want.''

''No, my traveling days are over. The last two months have been some of the best of my life. Now I'd rather stay on Snowbird with you and Nia and spend every Christmas as we've done this year.''

''That suits me just fine.''

''We should get back. Your family won't eat without us, and I don't want to spoil their dinner.''

''*Our* family,'' he corrected her.

She smiled with joy. ''Yes, our family. They're probably waiting for us.''

They locked the center and drove home. As they got out, she could hear laughter from inside Annie's. She halted at the bottom of the steps.

''Something wrong?'' Ryan asked.

''No, something's very right. I'm imagining all the wonderful Christmases we'll have together. Nia helping me decorate the barn. The family gathered at the table for dinner. Yesterday, I was desolate. Today, I have so much to look forward to.''

''We both do.''

''Nana Sipsey predicted I'd find a place for myself here. I think she always knew we'd end up together. Do you believe she really does have second sight?''

''I never did until now.''

''I wonder if all her prophesies come true.''

''My mother says so.''

Susannah thought about another of Nana's visions—Nia surrounded by many brothers and sisters, two with identical faces.

''Do twins run in your family?''

''Yeah, my mother's a twin. Aunt Eileen lives in Texas.''

''How do you feel about having more children? Lots and lots of children?''

His eyebrows lifted. ''Fine…I guess.''

She slipped her arm in his and smiled. ''Maybe you should start getting used to the idea.''

COOPER'S CORNER

Welcome to Twin Oaks—
the new B and B in Cooper's Corner.
Some come for pleasure, others for
passion—and one to set things straight...

Coming in January 2003...
ACCIDENTAL FAMILY
by Kristin Gabriel

Check-in: When former TV soap star Rowena Dahl's biological clock started ticking, she opted to get pregnant at a fertility clinic. Unfortunately, she got the wrong sperm!

Checkout: Publisher Alan Rand was outraged that a daytime diva was having *his* baby. But he soon realized that he wanted Rowena as much as he wanted their child.

HARLEQUIN®

Makes any time special ®

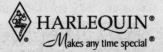

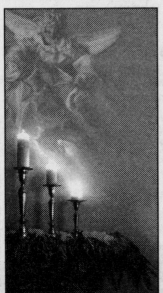

HARLEQUIN *Super*ROMANCE®

presents a compelling family drama—
an exciting new trilogy
by popular author Debra Salonen

THOSE SULLIVAN SISTERS

Jenny, Andrea and Kristin Sullivan are much more
than sisters—*they're triplets!* Growing up as one of
a threesome meant life was never lonely...or dull.

Now they're adults—with separate lives, loves,
dreams and secrets. But underneath everything that
keeps them apart is the bond that holds them together.

MY HUSBAND, MY BABIES
(Jenny's story)
available December 2002

WITHOUT A PAST
(Andi's story)
available January 2003

THE COMEBACK GIRL
(Kristin's story)
available February 2003

HARLEQUIN®
Makes any time special ®

Visit us at www.eHarlequin.com

HSRTSS